KEEPING her WET

USA TODAY BESTSELLING AUTHOR

M. ROBINSON

VIP

Ysabelle & Sebastian

CHAPTER ONE

Ysabelle

My eyes closed as I sank into the fizzing bubbles, feeling the tension release with every sinking inch. The heat permeated my skin, relaxing the tightness in my lower back and shoulders. Taking a deep breath, the lavender steam filled my senses, and I sighed in contentment.

Happy for the moment of alone time.

"Moooom!"

Pinching the thin part of my nose, I groaned, "What, Lilah? You're supposed to be in bed."

"My daddy say no."

I pulled in my lips to keep from laughing at her. Once that happened, I was done. She was hard-headed like her father without giving her any ammunition. The last thing I wanted was to start a battle with this little monkey, especially when Sebastian wasn't

3

home yet. He'd let her get away with murder. She could do no wrong in his eyes, which is why most of her replies started with, "My daddy say no."

"Your daddy isn't home yet. That's why Mommy's bubble bath is being interrupted. Again. What do you need now, Lilah?"

My three-year-old teenager wobbled into the bathroom with her messy bedhead and pink princess pajamas. "Me have a bad dream."

Sighing, "You need to be sleeping in order for that to happen."

"The monster is under my bed. He gonna get me, again."

"Lilah, we talked about this. There is no monster under your bed. Go back in your room, I'll be right there to tuck you in again in a few minutes. Let me get dry."

"But the monster, Momma. He gonna—" We heard the garage door opening and that's all it took for Lilah's eyes to light up, knowing it was her father. Just like that, she was gone. My cool bubbles and I had been replaced by the love of her life in the blink of an eye.

"Daddy!" She didn't give me a second thought and took off as fast as her chubby little legs could carry her.

I shook my head, stifling a laugh. Grabbing my black silk robe from the back of the bathroom door, I put it on, making my way behind her. A laugh escaped my lips when I heard her giggle, jumping into her daddy's arms.

"Hey, princess. What are you still doing up?" Sebastian asked, kissing the top of her head as she held him tight against her tiny frame.

"Daddy, the monster under my bed is back. He gonna get me. I scared," she whimpered, tucking her head into the nook of his neck. Nestling up closer to him, allowing him to hold her tighter.

"I see."

This was all Sebastian ever wanted. It was like he was born to be a father. He was the best one I'd ever seen. Sometimes I thought he was a better parent than I was, he was just a natural at it.

He walked them over to the counter and sat her up on the edge. Kissing the top of her head one last time before grabbing her chin, making her look up with those puppy dog eyes that did it to him every time.

"I sleep wif you, otay?"

"Princess, remember we talked about this? There are no monsters under your bed. I check every night just to make sure."

"They leave and comes back when you gone, Daddy."

He sighed, glancing over at me for the first time. Arching an eyebrow when he saw me leaning against the wall, still wet and amused. My silk robe clinging to my curves, leaving little to the imagination.

"Sorry, I'm late. We ended up spearing more fish as the sun was going down," he explained, never taking his eyes off my body.

"Did your group have fun?"

5

"Don't they always?"

I laughed. "The restaurant was packed today. I'm exhausted, babe. I—"

"Go to bed. I got her," he interrupted, looking up at me.

As much as I hated leaving them, my body was just done. Don't get me wrong, life on the island was amazing, both our businesses were flourishing, but at times we could barely keep up. Sebastian added a few more charters and captains to his company. I opened up two more restaurants on other parts of the island. Adding Lilah into the mix was proving to be taxing, and our once steaming hot sex life had taken the biggest hit of all.

"I love you," I stated, wishing I could keep my eyes open long enough to spend a little more time with him.

"I love you, too. I'll be in as soon as I can."

Which meant he would fall asleep in Lilah's bed like he did on most nights when she woke up. He was adamant about not letting her sleep in our bed, so he always took her back to hers and ended up passing out in there, nonetheless. He was just as exhausted as I was.

No sooner than I had closed my eyes, I smelled his intoxicating scent hovering above me. The caress of his callused fingers stroked the side of my face.

"Watching me sleep is still stalkerish, Sebastian," I mumbled while opening my eyes. Teasing him with an old but familiar joke.

He laughed, wiggling out of his shirt, taking off his pants and sliding in behind me. His fingers immediately dug into my tense shoulders while his lips found my back, instantly reminding me why I loved him so much.

"Oh, God. Don't ever stop doing that," I moaned, loving the way his fingers deeply massaged my sore muscles.

My eyes began to shut more and more with each second that passed between us. Until I couldn't hold them open any longer and passed the hell out.

SEBASTIAN

"Daddy, I'm gonna miss you and Momma. Why can't I go agains?" Lilah questioned, cocking her cute little face to the side. Sitting up on the counter, watching me cook her breakfast.

She reminded me so much of Ysabelle. I resisted the urge to tell my wife how much I wanted another baby almost every night. Especially now that Lilah was getting older.

"Because who will play with Devon and Brooke?"

"Oh yeah! They needs me." She nodded happily, understanding.

I chuckled, setting her plate of food in front of her. I took a seat and listened intently to everything she shared with me, not letting me get a word in. Moments like that reminded me how much I loved our time together.

When I was finished with my plate, I left Lilah with the nanny, needing to wake up Ysa. She would sleep all morning if I let her.

"Mmm... five more minutes," she grumbled into the pillow, throwing the sheet above her head when she heard the door shut behind me.

I didn't think twice about it. I slid underneath the blankets in a slow, steady stride, crawling my way toward her pussy like a starved man. Before she knew what I was doing, my face was in between her legs.

"Sebastian," she breathed out as soon as I sucked on her clit, long and hard. Her hands pulled at my hair while her back arched off the bed seconds later.

"Lilah?" she simply stated, grinding her pussy into my mouth.

"You like that, baby? Does that feel good? Huh? Tell me, tell me it feels good," I huskily urged, ignoring her question. "Don't worry about Lilah. Just lay back and let me fucking eat you."

Her hands began fisting the sheets, and I had barely started touching her yet. My mouth already sending her body into a frenzy. I was being gentle with her, taking my time to devour her sweet pussy, making her nice and wet for me. Sucking her clit side-to-side, forcefully, urgently back and forth, up and down. Pulling back the hood of her clit till her legs started to shake from just the mere graze of my tongue. I knew her body better than she did.

She was almost fucking there.

"Oh God," she whimpered in pleasure, throwing the sheets off both of our bodies.

My hands moved their way up to her breasts, kneading her hard nipples, lapping at her pussy, and eating her like she was my favorite fucking meal. Making her go crazy with passion and desire.

Feelings only I could ever produce.

I licked her one last time before stopping. Peering up at her with hooded eyes, I ordered, "Let's go."

Her eyes widened, shaking her head no.

I grinned. "If you're a good girl. I will finish what I started later."

"Sebastian, this is bull—"

My tongue was in her mouth, shutting her the hell up before she got the last word out. Making her savor the taste of herself all over my lips and tongue. I grabbed onto the back of her neck, pulling her closer to me. Placing her exactly where I wanted her.

Completely underneath me.

She licked and sucked on my tongue, panting, moaning, and scratching at me to keep going.

I didn't.

Instead, I abruptly grabbed a fistful of her hair, causing her to yelp from the sudden intrusion on her scalp. "Let's go," I demanded in a much harsher tone, not wanting to have my way with her just yet.

I had other plans that involved her being in a string bikini, completely at my mercy.

Uninterrupted.

I kissed her one last time before letting her go and getting off the bed. Adjusting my hard cock and balls in my jeans once I was standing.

"You got five minutes to get dressed and packed, or we're leaving without it," I informed, leaving her wet, naked, and wanting.

I walked into Lilah's room, thanking Devon and Brooke for coming to stay with her for a few days on such short notice. I needed time with my wife. I wanted to spend a few days with her, just us.

Alone.

I wanted to fuck her seven ways to Sunday, in every last corner of my new 50-foot Viking yacht. She didn't even know I'd bought it for her.

For us.

Ysabelle was walking toward Lilah's room with her bag in hand as I was walking out, shutting the door behind me.

I shook my head no, stopping her dead in her tracks. "Lilah sees you, she's going to throw a goddamn fit. We don't have time for meltdowns if you want to continue what I started. And by the look on your face, I know you can't wait to have my face deep in your pussy. Fucking you with my mouth." I closed the distance between us, taking her bag from her. "She's fine. I said goodbye to her for you. I'm sure she will be all too eager to Facetime with you later."

"Sebastian, this is—" Placing her bag on the floor next to me, I pulled out a black tie from the pocket of my jeans. Rendering her speechless, I walked behind her, wrapping the tie around her eyes so she couldn't see.

Whispering in her ear, "Do you trust me?"

Her breathing hitched. "With my life."

I smiled at her response, picked up her bag, and grabbed her hand, leading her out to the garage. I helped her down into my Ferrari, sliding on her seatbelt, and kissing her luscious lips one last time before closing the door.

"So are you going to tell me where we're going? Because I'm pretty sure this is considered kidnapping," she said, breaking the silence between us as I pulled out of the driveway.

"It's not kidnapping if it belongs to you, Ysa."

She smirked, leaning her head back against the headrest. Relaxing for the first time in God knows how long.

We pulled up to the marina about two hours later. I planned to island hop for the next few days so I had the captain I hired meet us closer out to sea.

After getting Ysabelle out of the car, I picked her up unexpectedly, hurling her over my shoulder, once again leading us to our final destination. Throwing her into a fit of giggles.

"Where are we going?" she questioned, realizing I was taking us somewhere else.

"Where I can have my way with you." I spanked her ass, stepping onto the yacht and nodding to the captain to take off again, silently ordering the crew to leave, too.

I placed her down on the ground, removing her blindfold. Her eyes fluttered open, adjusting to the bright light all around her.

"Oh my God!" she shouted, surprised to see a whole spread of breakfast on the back table. She grabbed some fruit, making her way inside. I followed close behind her, wanting to see the look on her face as she took in her new surroundings. "Whose yacht is this?"

"Yours," I simply replied.

She glanced over at me. "What?"

I grinned, loving the way her eyes lit up from my simple response. I shook off the sentiment, grabbing her hand again, and leading her toward the front bow. Nodding to the side once we were standing in the perfect spot.

She leaned over, taking in the name.

"You named her after me!" she shouted, immediately turning around and jumping into my arms. Much like our daughter always did. "I can't believe you did this! Lilah is going to love it. You know how—" I kissed her, silencing her.

"No more talking about Lilah. For the next few days, you're all mine. Do you understand me? Just Ysa. My wife. My VIP."

She laughed so hard her head fell back. "Oh… is that what this is about? You want me to be your whore? Well, I hate to burst your bubble, but you couldn't afford me."

"I did once before," I reminded, even though it brought back bad memories.

For her.

She was always fucking mine.

"I'm more expensive now."

"Is that so?"

She proudly nodded. "You see, Mr. Vanwell. I discovered the love of a man. It's going to take a lot more than just money for me to spread my legs for you."

I backed us into the bow wall, pressing her up against it with my right arm locking her in place by the side of her face. While my other hand went right for the inside of her thigh, her short cotton dress making it easy for me to do so.

"You had the love of a man back then, too," I recapped, kissing down the side of her neck. My fingers grazing higher and higher up her long, silky legs.

"That's not how I remember it."

"Are you trying to provoke me?"

"Maybe."

"You don't need to provoke me to make me fuck you, Ysa. I've wanted to fuck that saucy little mouth since this morning."

She sucked in air, startled by what I'd just said. I continued my gentle torture for a few more seconds, moving closer to where she wanted me to touch her the most. I brought my other hand up, grazing her cheek with the tips of my fingers, placing a fallen piece of her hair behind her ear.

The gesture made her lips part.

"I thought I'd take you out for a ride. Don't you want to ride me, baby?" I asked, purposely trailing my fingers down the slit of her pussy. "You're beautiful when you blush like that." I lightly brushed my fingertips further down her slit, gliding them into her opening. "I love how fucking wet you always are for me."

Our gazes stayed connected the entire time, her eyes showing me everything I wanted to hear. Even after all these years, they still spoke volumes. I cocked my head to the side and stepped in toward her, it didn't take much for my mouth to be close to hers. I pulled her closer to me by the nook of her neck, and she didn't cower. If anything she stood taller.

She bit her bottom lip, enticing me, using her sexuality. Reminding me exactly why she was the best VIP.

Ysabelle was made for sex.

I started to move my fingers, aiming them directly toward her g-spot. "No one can see us out here," I whispered close enough to her mouth that I could feel her breath upon my lips. "But does it excite you that someone could walk out and see us? You'd let me fuck you right here and now, wouldn't you?"

"I was never one for being shy."

I gripped the front of her neck, my thumb and index finger clutching her pulse points. "No one sees what's mine but *me*. I know what you feel like when you come. I know that your face gets flushed. I know you stop breathing just slightly before your pussy starts to pulsate so fucking tight that it pushes my fingers out." I bit her bottom lip and then kissed her softly. "I know what you taste like. What you feel like being wrapped around my cock all night long."

She swallowed the saliva that had pooled in her mouth. Her breathing elevated, showing me that I was getting to her. I slid my middle finger out from her hot cunt, bringing it up to her lips, and running it along her pouty bite. Enjoying the feel of her slickness against my callused fingers.

"That's how fucking wet I make you," I growled, licking her lips clean. Needing to taste her with an urgency I felt every single day.

She was like a drug to me. Since day one. I couldn't ever get enough.

I was addicted.

She kissed me, soft at first, testing the feel of my mouth on hers. Seeing if I would respond the way she wanted me to and I didn't. I wouldn't. The way her lips claimed mine told me she wanted me to make the first move, so I did, but not with her mouth.

With her pussy.

I pushed my middle and ring fingers back into her wet pussy and she moaned into my mouth, shoving her tongue in at the exact same moment. Letting me savor both the taste and feel of her. How her body angled perfectly beneath mine. She melted against me, taking everything I was giving her and wanting more.

Wanting everything.

"Do you want me to fuck you?" I said in between kisses. "Do you want me to make you come?

Silence.

"Tell me…" I urged, pushing my fingers deeper into her sweet spot.

She panted, "Right there."

"Where?" I cocked my head to the side, still not moving our lips apart. "Here?"

"Yes…"

"Tell me."

"I love you," she moaned, trying to glide her tongue back into my mouth. I jerked back, not allowing her that satisfaction.

Not yet.

She whimpered in disapproval, craving my mouth, my taste, her taste. Her pussy betrayed her, tightening around my fingers. Releasing her juices that slid down the palm of my hand. So close to coming apart.

She shuddered, her body quivering.

"One," I pointed out.

I loved her pussy.

I loved the taste of it.

I loved the feel of it.

I loved the smell of it.

I love her.

Not allowing her to recover, I got down on my knees, taking her clit into my mouth. Her body started to convulse all around my face. The hood of her clit pulled back exposing her fucking bright red nub, all I had to do was take it into my mouth and suck.

Hard.

She was so fucking wet, I bathed in her salty, musky, sweetness, rubbing my face all over her pussy. Drenching my lips and my five o'clock shadow. I lapped at her, never taking my persistent tongue away from her clit, making her squirm to no avail. Her juices dripped down my face, to my throat, and onto my chest, soaking into my white button-down shirt. The taste of her would linger in my mouth for hours, allowing me to savor the way I made her pussy come. I loved nothing more than to rub her juices all around my lips, fingers, or cock and then wipe them all around her beautiful face.

I loved hearing her moan, whimper, and her breath quicken. I loved the way she was struggling to catch her bearings as my tongue danced from her clit to her opening, and back to her clit again.

She literally fucked my face.

Coming over and over again.

Her shaking legs couldn't hold her up any longer, her weight falling heavy on my face, her hands tangling in my hair. I threw her over my shoulder again, smacking her ass, stating, "Two, three, and four." The number of times I made her come on my tongue.

I placed her ass on the counter in the kitchen of the yacht, but she didn't stay on there long. Sliding down the length of my body, she got down on her knees in front of me, pulling out my hard fucking cock from my jeans. She licked off the pre-come, sucking the head into her mouth. Taking me in inch-by-inch.

With her body beneath mine and my dick hovering above her mouth, I thrust in and out of her swollen lips. Her pouty mouth taking my dick as I shoved it to the back of her throat, making her gag, spit falling down the sides of her face.

"Fuck... I need to be inside of you."

Her eyes watered with tears, but she didn't let up. I enjoyed the feel of her lips wrapped around my cock and her taking every last inch I had to give. Removing my cock from her mouth with a pop, she aggressively sucked in the air that my dick denied her.

I didn't falter. Grabbing her underneath the arms, I carried her up the length of my body and pulled off her dress and panties before I lifted her to me. Slamming her down onto my rock hard shaft in one swift, sudden movement.

"Jesus, Sebastian. You're so fucking big."

I took it easy on her at first, letting her get used to the size and girth of my cock as she slid up and down, effortlessly panting. Her mouth parted and her soft, wet tongue peeked out. She bit her bottom lip while trying to keep her eyes open. I took in her soft glow, her rosy cheeks, and the subtle sweat pooling at her temples. I watched the way her tits bounced, the way her back would curve, and how she arched just slightly at the last second of feeling my balls swaying against her ass cheeks.

I walked us back to the bedroom, laying down on the bed with her now on top of me. She rode my dick slow and steady, and I let her feel like she was in control, which was a bunch of bullshit.

I was.

I always am.

I smacked her ass hard, and her eyes widened in surprise and delight while I gripped onto her ass cheeks, making her ride me harder and faster.

Ysabelle loved to be manhandled, she loved to feel owned, and I gladly gave it to her.

"Fuck me, baby. Fuck me like you want me to fuck you." I clutched the back of her neck and brought her to me. She leaned forward, and I could feel her g-spot on the tip of my cock, causing me to inadvertently groan in satisfaction.

"You smell that? Hmmm? You smell yourself all over my fucking face?"

"Yes," she breathed out as I rotated my hips in the opposite direction of hers.

"Lick it off," I ordered, causing her eyes to widen again. I gripped her harder, placing her closer to my mouth where the smell of her come and cherry lip-gloss lingered.

She grinned and her pink velvety tongue poked out, sliding from my top lip to my chin. She innocently smiled, leaning back to ride me harder and more demanding. I wiped the residue off my face with the palm of my hand and smeared it all over her gorgeous face.

She bit my fingers when I moved them to her mouth and began to eagerly suck them clean. This woman was my undoing. I flipped us over, placed her legs on my shoulders, and pounded the fuck out of her tight, wet pussy… in and out. Holding myself up around her head.

"Who fucks you good, baby? I won't stop until I have you screaming my name, Ysa."

I heard the slapping sound of my balls against her soft, wet skin and leaned back to spread her legs wide open. Wanting to watch my cock take her perfect goddamn cunt. Claiming what I knew had always been fucking mine.

She helplessly, breathlessly repeated, "Yes… yes… yes…"

A growl surfaced loud from deep within my chest, she was so fucking tight it made my balls ache. Manipulating her clit with my fingers, her legs started to tremble, caging my body in. I thrust in and out of her, never letting up on fucking her, grabbing onto her breasts, roughly caressing her hard nipples. The firmness of my grasp was evident from her bright, red skin. I smacked it a few times, knowing it would leave a mark. I growled and held her down, moving her up and down on my cock until she begged me to stop.

I never did.

I never do.

The smell of her arousal and come was all around us. Her whole body tightened so fucking hard, suffocating me in nothing but her need to come. I knew every goddamn button my wife had, what made her purr, moan, pant, sweat, tremble, and tighten.

It wasn't the orgasm I was after…

I wanted the climax.

I wanted the build up.

I wanted the wetness.

Her pussy pulsated and clamped onto my cock, pushing me out of her wet, warm fucking heat.

But most of all, I loved to fucking watch…

The way she would squirm.

The way she would sweat.

The way she would hold her breath, right before falling over the brink of ecstasy. Taking every last bit of pleasure she could.

"Sebastian! Yes… yes… Sebastian!"

Coming with everything she had.

The way she took her pleasure with everything I made her feel.

My balls throbbed with the need to come from watching her climax.

"I fucking love you," I groaned out, emptying my balls deep into her pussy. Looking her straight in the eyes, I huskily demanded, "Give me another baby."

She smiled, big and wide and announced, "I'm pregnant."

the Madam

Mika, Madam & Martinez

CHAPTER TWO

**DISCLAIMER: If you have read El Diablo—
this is prior to Martinez and Lexi.**

MIKA

"Angel, ask yourself… Do you honestly think I give a flying fuck about *El Diablo*?" I questioned, arching an eyebrow. Kicking my feet up on her desk, grinning as I folded my arms over my chest.

Her gaze narrowed, only eyeing my combat boots. I crossed one leg over the other, nestling in my seat, getting nice and fucking comfortable. I don't know why she always thought she could go toe-to-toe with me, knowing she was just another bitch, not the alpha dog she claimed to be.

"Don't fuck this up for me, Mika," she warned in a harsh tone as if it made a fucking difference.

Her bark was always much bigger than her fucking bite.

"I wouldn't fucking dream of it," I mocked, surrendering my hands up in the air.

"I'm serious. I don't even know why you're here. Don't you have someone else's skirt to poke your head up?"

"Jealous?"

"I'm not the one who is sitting in your office like a little, lost puppy, waiting on you. Now am I?" She sat back in her chair, slowly crossing her long, silky legs. Tapping her manicured fingernails on the leather armrests.

"I just want to know what all the fuss is about? Can't a man meet his competition?"

She snidely smiled. "There was never any competition."

"No shit, baby. We both know whose cock you belong to." I gestured toward mine. "Want me to get it nice and hard for you, angel? All you have to do is get on your knees, open your fucking mouth, and say please. I'll take care of the rest."

"I don't have time to play with you today, Mika. Now get the fuck out."

I didn't move an inch.

"Mika, I—" The door opened, immediately silencing her. Her intense glare instantly moved to the man behind me, who closed the door behind him.

I'd never seen her cower down to anyone other than me, and fuck did it make my cock hard.

I didn't bother turning around, I was much more interested in the woman who was practically batting her eyelashes at the man taking a seat beside me.

"Who the fuck is this dick? I wasn't aware you'd have company. What part of private meeting did you not understand, Lilith?" he inquired in a slight Spanish accent.

"Madam," she corrected not missing a beat.

"I'm Mika," I interrupted, answering for myself.

"Her bodyguard? Or just her bitch?"

"Says the man who's taking a meeting in The Madam's office."

"Mika," she warned. "Please excuse him, Martinez, he has so much to learn. He doesn't share well with others."

"Ah, just as I thought. That does make you her bitch." He grinned, leaning back into his chair.

"Angel, I don't need any introductions. I'm just here watching out for you. Can't be too careful nowadays with all these spics, crossing the border—"

"Call me a spic again, motherfucker. I'll put a bullet in the middle of your fucking forehead. Better yet, I'll have her do it." He nodded toward her.

I laughed. I couldn't help it.

"Enough!" she shouted, abruptly standing. Slamming her fists on her desk, bringing both of our attention back to her. "You two want to act like little boys, then do it on your own time. I'm not here to play mommy."

I'd known Lilith since she was eighteen-years-old. Almost eleven years now, and she still knew how to govern a goddamn room. It never mattered how many men she was surrounded by, there was something about her that brought them to their knees. If anything...

It made her fucking stronger.

She opened the top drawer of her desk, throwing a kilo of cocaine on the mahogany wood.

"You came for this." She gestured to the package. "Not to prove your cock was bigger than his. But take it from a woman who has seen both," she informed, smirking as she sat back down in her leather chair. "They're comparable."

"You fucked him?" I blurted. "Mr. Uptight Suit over here? Oh wait, I'm not surprised. You share your pussy with anyone and everyone."

She chuckled, "It's been a while. But a man never forgets his first, does he? El Diablo?" she mocked in a teasing tone.

I scoffed, "And the plot fucking thickens."

"And even back then... I was still paying for your goods." Martinez leaned forward, grabbing the blow. He poked a hole in the clear plastic with a key, bringing it up to his nose.

Inhaling long and hard.

I didn't waver. Leaning over, I snorted a huge rail off the table with Lilith not far behind me. I couldn't tell you where things started to take an unexpected turn. But I could tell you that the more fucked

25

up we got, the easier it was for me to tolerate the motherfucker. A few hours seemed to go by in a whirlwind of nothing but liquor and drugs, both flowing as freely as the pussy that ran rampant in The Cathouse.

I never expected what was fucking coming.

Or yes, yes I fucking did…

Madam

One minute I thought we were going to have a meeting to talk about the new cartel shipments. The next, we're all getting fucked up from the same cocaine I wanted Martinez to start pushing.

They both looked good enough to fucking devour. Two handsome as hell men sitting in my office, hanging on every word that left my red lips. Each grinning from ear-to-ear. Mika whispered something in Martinez's ear, and I couldn't help but think how much this reminded me of a few years back. Except Martinez wasn't his friend JJ, and this wasn't a setup.

At least I didn't think it was.

"You coming down, Angel?" Mika questioned, repeating the exact same words he did that night years ago.

My pussy clenched as he made his way toward me, looking like sex on a fucking stick. The same look that always made my heart beat faster and my pussy wet. I stood in the middle of my office, standing taller the closer he got to me.

Getting near my face, he murmured, "You smell like you want to be fucked, Lilith, do you want us to fuck you?" he baited in a sinful tone.

I smiled, big and wide. "You can't be serious."

"You know how many times I've thought about that night? How many times I've stroked my cock to the images of watching my boy fuck you? How much I remember the way your asshole felt while there was a cock deep inside your wet, fucking cunt? You see… I don't mind sharing because I know who you fucking belong to. Who am I to deny you of such pleasure? When I fuck more VIPs than I know what to do with… You know I like to watch, angel. You're my favorite fucking thing to watch."

My chest rose and fell with each word that fell from his lips. I perched myself forward to try to kiss him, but he teasingly moved his head away. Roughly gripping onto the back of my hair by the nook of my neck, tugging back ever so slightly. Making me yelp from the sudden intrusion.

"Your body is mine to do with as I please, it always has been. It's why you keep coming back for more, angel. There's no one who can fuck you like I can… except maybe *him*?"

My eyes shifted toward Martinez who was still sitting back in his chair, calm, cool and fucking collected.

"Are you challenging me, motherfucker?" he baited, giving Mika exactly what he wanted. Sending shivers coursing down my spine.

"Don't pretend like you haven't paid for a VIP, Martinez. Little did you know that Lilith here... The Madam is the best. Trust me, I would know. I've fucked them all. With and without her watching, let alone her consent."

Martinez narrowed his eyes at me. "Doesn't it bother you that he fucks other women?"

"I know whose pussy he belongs to," I mocked Mika, throwing his words back at him. Only looking at him.

"Neither of us are one's for being monogamous. But angel here... doesn't get to play that often since she's taken over as Queen Fucking B. I enjoy watching her get fucked quite a bit. I mean look at her, she's like a goddamn bitch in heat. It's one of the things I love the most about her. Always willing, ready, and soaking fucking wet... tell him, Lilith, tell him how much you love getting fucked in every hole," Mika roared in a domineering, yet sexy tone that made my pussy clench.

Martinez stood, walking up in front of me. Stopping when he was inches away from my face. "You trust me enough to let me fuck you in the culo?" Martinez inquired with lust and determination laced in his voice.

"Mmm hmm," I moaned, closing my eyes.

Waiting.

"Get on your fucking knees," Mika ordered, shoving me down to the floor in one rough movement.

Mika loved to claim that he was the only one who could ever order me around, in and out of the bedroom. I would be lying if I said he was wrong.

I hated it as much as I loved it.

Especially right now.

"I'll reward you when you fucking earn it. Now pull out his cock and show me just how good of a deep throating whore you are."

I smiled from ear-to-ear and happily obliged.

They wanted a VIP then I'd give them The fucking Madam.

MIKA

She pulled out his already hard cock, immediately licking down the sides, caressing his balls at the same time. Humming when she sucked the head of his dick into her mouth, never letting up on stroking his shaft and playing with his sack.

A man like Martinez could appreciate the fucking beauty of the situation unfolding in front of him. And by that I mean the woman on her knees, deep throating his cock like the whore she would always be.

Angel's pleasure always came before mine.

No matter what.

My pleasure was to watch my girl get fucked, but my pain wasn't far behind. Watching another man take what was mine took a lot more restraint than one might think. In the end, it didn't matter because I was the only man who had fucked my way into her cold, calculated heart.

We were one and the same.

"Deeper," I ordered, grabbing ahold of her hair by the nook of her neck. Forcing her to do as I said.

Martinez groaned, watching as I pushed her deeper down his shaft. She couldn't get half of it in her mouth, but he appreciated the gesture nonetheless. She greedily took every last inch of it. Just watching made my own cock twitch in my jeans. He thrust in and out, pumping faster, harder strokes. She kept up the pace as firm as she could, making her mouth a fucking vise for him.

"Asi, puta," Martinez said in Spanish. "Dámelo," he grunted through gritted teeth, grabbing a handful of hair on the top of her head.

I crouched down behind her, tightening my grip on the back of her neck harder and more demanding. "I'm going to fuck your wet cunt with my fingers, angel, and you're going to come all over them. You're going to ride my hand as you continue to suck his cock. Showing him just how good you're going to ride his dick next."

I pulled up her pencil shirt, groaning when I saw the lace of her black thigh-highs and the black garters holding them up. Pleased to find she wasn't wearing any panties.

She never did.

I licked my fingers, deciding to spit on them at the last second before placing them on her clit. Earning me the heady moan that escaped her chest.

"Don't stop sucking him off. Disobey me and watch what fucking happens."

She didn't. She followed my orders the exact way I knew she would. I pushed my middle and ring fingers readily inside of her. Aiming right for her g-spot. Pumping my fingers faster with each stroke of her mouth devouring Martinez's cock.

"Fuck her face, Martinez. This bitch likes it rough. Do what you want to her. For tonight... she's *ours*," I said, emphasizing the last word.

Martinez roughly grabbed ahold of the sides of her face, the gentleness he was showing her up until that point ceased to exist any longer. I gave him free rein to do what he wanted. Unleashed a whole other side of the motherfucker.

And a man like him appreciated that from a man like me.

I was going to do what I fucking pleased.

We both were.

I'd make sure of it.

She started to rock her hips, trying to relieve the ache that I was creating. Unable to beg me for it with her mouth full of cock, like she knew I loved.

"You want us to fuck that beautiful, glistening cunt don't you, Lilith? You're dripping wet just waiting for our cocks to sink into

31

your fucking heat. You want us to fuck you so deep in your pussy and asshole that you won't be able to walk for days. Every time you move, you can still feel us there. That's what you want, isn't it?" I questioned, making her crave exactly what I was saying.

Madam

I could physically feel my pussy pushing Mika's fingers out. My heat clamping down as a wave of ecstasy rushed through me. It didn't take long until I felt him rimming the pucker of my asshole with my own come. Gradually easing one in, as his other fingers continued to fuck my cunt. Fucking each of my holes simultaneously. It was only a matter of minutes before my body was convulsing, contracting, and shaking, which made Martinez thrust in and out of my mouth even harder and faster. It was all too much, an overload of emotions and sensations.

Mika found my g-spot from the inside of my asshole and didn't let up, finger fucking me with full force.

"That's the spot right there, isn't it, angel? I knew I could find it even fucking a different hole. Should I let her come, motherfucker?" He looked up to Martinez with a fucking smirk.

Martinez ignored him, releasing my mouth with a loud pop, causing me to come with so much pressure that my entire body quivered and trembled.

I saw fucking stars, needing to shut my eyes tight.

"No, hijo de puta," Martinez finally replied. "That one was all mine."

They both stared at each other, silently challenging one another to a pissing contest. Whose cock was bigger and who was going to make me come the most. All I knew was, I was about to be fucked. Literally.

Mika picked me up as if I weighed nothing, throwing me onto the couch. They took the opportunity to undress me. Taking off my clothes with an urgency and speed I hadn't felt since the first time I did this with Mika and JJ. I was left in only my thigh-highs, garter belt, and heels. When I came down from the high, I opened my eyes, seeing exactly what I had pictured in my mind. Both men on their knees, stroking their cocks with excitement in their dark, dilated glares.

Staring only at me.

I grinned at them, watching the way their hands glided along their glorious shafts.

Easing my way back down onto the leather ottoman, which was more like a bed. Lying on my back, I spread my legs as wide as they would go as an open invitation for them to do what they pleased. They took ahold of my feet and started to caress them, eliciting a gasp from deep within my core, causing my back to arch off the cool surface. A trail of heat instantly overtook my body, awakening sensations and desires only Mika could ever accomplish.

They moved simultaneously together, it was if they didn't need to communicate with words. Between each other, they knew what we all wanted. Moving in sync up my calves to my thighs, kneading and rubbing their way toward my pussy.

I silently repeated, "Please, don't stop," in my head over and over again, afraid that if I said it out loud they would halt, just to torture me. The touch of their hands continued to caress my limbs, igniting my nerve endings into a smoldering fire.

Martinez moved in between my legs and Mika came to my side. He started to caress my breasts in a soft, but demanding touch, down to the sides of my stomach. I sat up and crawled toward Martinez. He obliged, lying back as I slid my way up his solid, muscular torso, loving the feel of his skin against my nails. The smell of his cologne immediately assaulted my senses, consuming me in ways I never experienced before. Mika came up from behind me, pushing my breasts down on Martinez's dick, cupping them and silently signaling him to jerk forward and backward in between them. Fucking my tits with ease.

"Fuck them titties," Mika encouraged, pushing me further.

Martinez obliged, swaying his hips in a sultry dance. I stuck out my tongue to get a taste. Lapping at his dick like a goddamn ice cream with every push upward. He groaned in satisfaction. Pleased with his whore.

Mika laid back on the couch, propping himself up, tugging me with him. He was never one for sharing too long. My back set to his front, our bodies sticking together. Martinez wasn't far behind, settling himself once again between my legs. Mika kissed his way up my back, playing with the pucker of my asshole, making slow, torturous circles. I grabbed the back of Mika's head and hastily pulled him toward me. Craning my neck, kissing him with hunger and craving more. The feeling of having his lips tangled with mine enhanced every single response from my sex.

I wanted and needed more.

"Bien," Martinez ordered, "Come" in Spanish, and I willingly went.

Straddling his thighs on my knees, as he leaned back supporting his weight on his hands. I bent forward, stroking Martinez's cock with my hand in a twirling motion. He grunted, taking one of his hands and started to make torturous circles around my clit, my nub peeking out once again. Mika positioned his face near my ass and unceasingly fucked my asshole with his finger. Soon replacing it with his tongue, licking the pucker with abandonment, shoving his tongue as deep as it would go.

"Fuck, it's been so long. I forgot what this sweet ass tasted like. Spread your legs wider, sweetheart. I'm fucking going in deep this time." He did. Plunging his tongue in and out as Martinez manipulated my nub. I didn't know which felt better, but I rode them both equally.

Martinez pushed two fingers into my wet heat, aiming straight for my g-spot while Mika continued to tongue fuck my asshole, switching it off between his fingers and tongue. I watched with hooded eyes as Martinez rolled on a condom. The raw uninhibited craving to want to come again hit me like a ton of fucking bricks. Before my core contracted and I knew what was happening, Martinez stood taking me with him. Wrapping my legs around his waist, he slammed his cock into me as Mika simultaneously shoved his cock into my ass. Each hole they were just fucking with their fingers, was now occupied by their dicks, making me scream out in pleasure.

I felt full, whole, and complete. I slowly but purposely moved my hips, and Mika gently guided himself out and back in.

"Jesus Christ… you're so fucking tight," Martinez rumbled.

"Tell him how much you love my cock in your ass," Mika lured, his voice full of yearning.

"Oh, God, please don't stop. You guys are so fucking hot. Fuck me harder, faster… yes… ahhh… yes… yes…just like that," I praised as they both fucked me at the same time and pace.

"You're such a fucking whore. You love having your ass and cunt fucked at the same time," Mika growled, loud and needy.

Their cocks were getting thicker and harder, and I swear they felt bigger. It made my pussy pulsate, gripping even tighter. Mika caressed my breasts and pinched my nipples, and Martinez started teasing my clit with one hand, both men supporting my weight. My head fell back on Mika's shoulder, and he nipped and sucked on my neck, saying dirty, filthy things that pushed me closer to the edge.

"It doesn't matter how many men fuck you, angel. Your ass, your cunt, your fucking heart... it belongs to me. I own you. Every last fucking part of you."

I moaned into his mouth.

Martinez suddenly pulled out, making me whimper from the loss of pressure. Mika slowed his movements, still filling my ass to the rim.

"Awe, angel," he mocked, using Mika's nickname for me. Cocking his head to the side. "You want more? You want me to let you come, don't you?"

I nodded, biting my lip to the point of pain, unable to speak.

"Like this?" He took his cock and slapped it against my swollen clit, making my ass cheeks clench Mika's dick.

"Hmmmm..." I moaned.

He slapped it again, not once but twice, making me come completely undone again. Falling to his knees, he began to consume my heat while I sat on his face, working my hips in sync with Martinez's tongue and Mika's shaft.

"I couldn't hear you, whore. Dime lo," he grumbled, his voice acting as a fucking vibrator between my legs.

"What's wrong, baby? Pussy got your tongue?" Mika nipped my earlobe and started to slowly pull out of my asshole. Martinez never let up.

"Fuck me…fuck me… fuck me…" I yelled, squirting all over Martinez's face. I could feel him grinning like the goddamn devil he was.

"Fuck, you taste good." He flicked my clit with his tongue a few more times before slamming his cock back into me.

"Don't stop. Never stop," I panted, everything becoming too much but not enough.

The room smelled of sex, lust, and cocaine. I couldn't believe how many times these two men had made me come, but my body still wanted more. All of our breathing and panting correlated. Nothing but the noise of bodies slapping together and sounds of pleasure filled the space. I don't know how long they fucked me. Each taking what they wanted and leaving me begging for more. Never wanting them to stop.

But like all good things, it was bound to end at some point.

They began to thrust faster and harder, filling me more and more. Then all of a sudden, I could feel we were all close. It took a few more thrusts and moans, and we all came at the exact same time. The men both emptied their seed deep within me. After pulling out, we all fell on top of each other's sweaty, slicked bodies.

The night had only just begun.

Brooke & Devon

CHAPTER THREE

Brooke

"Don't you want to play, Devon? I want to play," I said in the sultriest voice I could muster.

"Not falling for it, Bambi. I'm still fucking pissed at you."

"Devon! You can't stay mad at me this long! It's been forever!"

"It's been four hours."

"Those four hours, feel like four hundred. Come on... don't be mad at me." I crawled onto his lap on the couch. "I'm too adorable and pretty for you to be this upset with, please..." I pouted, giving him doe eyes.

Nothing.

"I said I was sorry. When people say they're sorry, you're supposed to forgive them. That's how it works. And then you're supposed to fuck them senseless so that they know you have forgiven them. Make-up sex."

"Is that how it works?"

I eagerly nodded.

He didn't falter. "What are you sorry for, Bambi?"

My eyes wandered all around the walls of our living room. We didn't live at The Cathouse since I took over as 'The Madam' a few years ago. Only going there when we needed to.

I couldn't even begin to tell you what I was supposed to be sorry for, I just knew he was pissed about something. Devon was extremely sensitive, even though he was such an alpha male. He liked to have things a certain way.

Especially when it came to me.

"I'm sorry I made you sad."

"Try again," he called me out. Already knowing I was full of shit.

I sucked in my bottom lip. This was not going as planned. My attention snapped back to the scene before me, and all I could see was impatience written all over his handsome face. I started to caress the side of his neck with my hand, and on the other side, I laid soft, tender kisses on his exposed skin. I continued my journey of touching and trying to seduce him to no avail.

"Devon… I love you. I'm sorry. Don't you love me?"

"Brooke, this has nothing to do with my love for you. Don't ever push my buttons thinking that you'll win by questioning my love for you."

I sighed, finally pulling away. Staring him straight in the eyes. "Okay... I'm sorry again."

"What are you sorry for in the first place?" he asked not backing down. Not that I thought he would.

I scratched the back of my head, feeling uneasy. Searching the walls once again for an answer. "Umm... see, here is the thing. I don't really know why..."

He didn't say a word, he barely even moved.

"I just know that you're upset with me, and I don't want you to be, that's all. I don't like it when you're mad at me, baby. Then I don't get laid. Even though the Incredible Hulk doesn't ever hate me," I teased, trying to lighten the situation. When that didn't work, I rocked my hips against his cock, wanting to prove my point. "He always loves me. Why don't you let me play with him? And then we'll all be friends again." I reached for his belt.

He grabbed my hands, stopping me.

"Oh my God! Why can't you just be a normal guy sometimes? Just let me suck your cock, give you a happy ending, then you'll stop being mad at me."

"I can't turn it on and off like you can, Brooke."

"I can turn it off?"

He narrowed his eyes, not amused with my banter in the least.

"Babe, sometimes I don't speak Devon, okay? Sometimes I just don't understand what the big deal is about, and sometimes you just confuse me. This is one of those times."

"Why not ask me first?" he simply replied, like it was the easiest thing to do in the world.

"Because I wanted to surprise you. I'm glad I told you about it before she was supposed to show up, though. You would have scared her away with all your huffing and puffing. Something would have been blown, and it wouldn't have been your cock."

"I don't like to play games. You, more than anyone else, should know that."

"You like to play my games I thought."

"Only if you run them by me first. Bambi, I don't need anyone other than you."

I smiled. I couldn't help it. "I know that. But she's a new VIP. I thought we could have a good time for the night. You know, like old times. Bring back some memories of the good ol' days," I paused to let my words sink in. "You do understand that I was bringing a VIP over to fuck you tonight, right? Just so we're clear."

"No. To fuck you."

"To fuck both of us," I clearly stated.

"Is there something you need? Something I'm not giving you? Because judging by how many times I make you come every day, you could understand why I'd be taken back."

I shook my head. "You give me everything I've ever wanted. I just thought... maybe... you would want to mix it up a bit. And since I have the capability of making that safely happen with smoking hot chicks, I might add... I don't know... it was a good idea in my head. I guess I just don't want you to ever get bored. I know we've been together for almost five years now, and you're the first relationship I've ever been in. So... I just want to keep you happy, especially sexually."

He nodded. Understanding finally passing through his gaze. "What made you think I'm not happy, Brooke? Do I not kiss you enough? Touch you enough? Fuck you enough? Tell me, how many times do I have to make you come in order for you to understand I'm truly happy?"

"Devon—" The doorbell rang, cutting me off. "Shit! With you being all mad at me, I may or may not have forgotten to tell her not to come." I winced, "I'm sorry. Again."

"Let her in." He nodded toward the front door.

"What?" I responded, confused by the turn of events.

"You heard me. Let her in. You want to play? Then I'm fucking game."

I didn't like the tone in his voice. Something was up. He was going to prove a point, I just wouldn't figure out what that was until I let her in.

DEVON

Never taking my eyes off of hers, I tugged on the seam of her purple panties, sliding them down her long, silky legs that went on for miles. She slipped one stiletto heel out, then the other. My fingers lightly skimmed the sides of her legs, leaving a trail of warmth behind.

Brooke watched my every move from the middle of the bed as I slowly, sensually worked over the new VIP, like I would normally do with her. Except this time, I hadn't taken my time with Brooke. I took off her clothes quickly and ordered her to go watch like the good little girl she always claimed to fucking be.

I was giving my full attention to the new whore, sitting spread eagle in front of me, willing and waiting for my next move. Brooke had an expression on her face I couldn't quite place, and quite frankly, I didn't give a flying fuck.

If she wanted to play then I would give her the game of a fucking lifetime.

I loved Brooke more than anything in this world, but honestly, I was so over her shit. There was only one way to make her understand, even if it meant I had to make love to someone else in front of her to make that happen. To get it through her thick, blonde skull that I didn't want anyone else.

"You're fucking gorgeous," I praised, kissing up her tan thighs. "What's your name, baby?"

"Whatever you want it to be," she whispered loud enough for us to hear.

I stood, leaning forward, resting my weight on my hands that were now on the sides of her face. Hovering above her tight, perfect body. Etching my lips on her collarbone, I blew soft breaths on her smooth skin giving her goose bumps. Feeling her breath catch as I lightly caressed the sides of her round, plump, perky breasts.

She stirred.

My luring breaths progressed to her tan, round, perfect nipples. I put my tongue on her left nipple and licked, and she moaned and grabbed the back of my neck, urging me to do more. With my teeth, I nipped it at first and then sucked, gently and then more firm. Once it was a hard pebble, I moved to her other breast and did the same. Peering up at her face, continuing to caress her breasts with my mouth and hands. My eyes moved from her face to her throat, seeing her pulse at the base of her neck.

Throbbing.

Her breathing started to elevate, getting heavier and heavier, causing her breasts to move upward every few seconds. Pushing them further into my mouth.

"Jasmine. I'll call you Jasmine," I declared, giving her a pet name that was part of the Disney franchise, like I had with Brooke who I'd lovingly named Bambi.

Speaking of the devil, I could feel her burning daggers into the sides of my face, and I resisted the urge to blurt out, "I thought you wanted to play?"

I went on, gradually kissing, licking, and sucking my way down her body. Making sure to touch and caress every last inch of her beautiful, brazen skin.

45

"Spread your legs, Jasmine," I ordered, in a soft tone.

She did as she was told, allowing my stocky frame to lie in between her thighs. I moved forward, causing her to move backward until she was fully lying down against our silk bed sheets. Her pussy straddled my thigh, and I immediately felt the moisture that had been pooling on her pussy, seeping through my jeans. She loudly gasped the second I lightly moved my thigh forward and backward on her clit. I did it a few times, getting rougher with the movement, spreading her juices up and down my leg.

My mouth moved in line with hers as she panted profusely. I started to trace her bottom lip with the tip of my tongue, following suit with the top. Softly pecking her lips to provoke a reaction.

Not from her.

From Brooke.

Jasmine understood my silent plea and opened her mouth. I didn't waver, plunging my tongue in, causing her to seek mine out.

"Please…" she purred against my lips. My mouth moved of its own accord until I got to her pussy. I could see she was fucking throbbing, craving for relief. She suppressed the urge to touch herself, her dainty fingers twitching at the sheets.

"I'm going to eat you now," I murmured against her wet heat, rubbing my nose up and down her clit, feeling the small bumps rising on her skin against my face. "I bet you fucking taste as good as you smell, sweetheart."

I nudged her clit with my nose one last time, casually kissing it. She moaned loudly, not taking her eyes off me. Wanting to watch my every move. I licked her from her opening to the top of her clit, sucking it in my mouth. Moving the soft nub back and forth and side-to-side, bringing my lips to an O shape, working her over. Getting her closer to the edge.

My fingers caressed her pussy, circling around her clit before thrusting into her tight opening. Her back arched off the bed, willing me to suck on her clit with more force as I manipulated the tip of my tongue to be in sync with my lips. Sucking and finger fucking her until she was moaning senselessly.

My stare purposely moved toward Brooke as Jasmine started coming apart on my tongue and against my fingers. We locked eyes for the first time since I took off Jasmine's clothes.

The look of pure jealousy radiated all around her, nothing of what she thought she would feel when she planned this little fucking fiasco.

I hated that I was hurting her.

But I needed to prove a point. I was getting too old for this fucking bullshit.

I wanted…

Needed…

Desired…

Only Brooke.

My Bambi.

I casually glided my way over to Brooke, staring her down as I crawled toward her. Leaving Jasmine to recover from her intense orgasm I'd just evoked. I backed Brooke onto the bed until her back hit the mattress, locking my arms around her head. Hovering above her in a predatory yet pissed off regard.

"Is this enough playtime for you?" I viciously spoke, kissing along her lips. Making her smell and taste Jasmine all along my face and mouth. "Do you want me to fuck her now? You tell me, Bambi... I'm just playing your game, remember?"

Brooke

I didn't pay any attention to what he was saying. I couldn't. I wanted him too much, just like he's always wanted me. I don't know why it took me to this point to understand what he meant by only wanting to be with me. If this was another place, another time, another man, then maybe it would have been different. I just wasn't this person anymore. We weren't this couple.

He was mine.

Only mine.

"I'm sorry," I breathed out, kissing him back. Hoping he would forgive me.

"What are you sorry for?" he repeated the same question as before.

"I'm sorry for making you feel like I wasn't good enough. I'm sorry for not trusting you. I'm sorry for trying to fix something that's never been broken. I'm just fucking sorry," I apologized, trying to hold back the tears.

He grinned, kissing my senseless. "I fucking love you. Just you."

"I know," I whispered, my voice breaking.

"Shhh… let me take care of you."

He looked over at Jasmine. "Go!" he ordered, she smirked, looking back and forth between us. A gleam in her eyes like she was witnessing something she'd never experienced before.

She grabbed her clothes off the floor and left.

"Come on," he ordered, standing and taking me with him.

He led me to the en suite bathroom, holding my hand the entire way. He turned on the faucets of the shower before stripping out of his clothes, disposing them on the floor. Grabbing my hand again, he stepped into our walk-in shower first. Shoving me up against the travertine wall with the rainfall showerheads cascading down all around us.

It was then I realized why he brought us in the shower. He wanted to wash off her scent and smell that lingered on his skin.

I couldn't love him more in that moment if I tried.

DEVON

"I love you," I repeated, kissing all along her face. The water drowned every last inch of our skin as if we were having sex under a waterfall.

I kissed my way down the side of her neck like I knew she loved, working my fingers on her clit. Kissing her collarbone, her breasts, sucking her nipples into my mouth.

She swayed her hips against my fingers, riding them, guiding them to grind against her clit. I pushed two fingers inside her pussy, still using the palm of my hand to rub her bundle of nerves.

"Your pussy feels so fucking tight. Come on my hand, give me what belongs to me."

Arching her back, her eyes rolled to the back of her head. I didn't let up, moving my fingers so fast, so deep inside her, wanting her to squirt down my hand. The sloshing sound of her come filled the space as I roughly finger fucked her, making her come undone in minutes.

Squirting over and over again.

I still didn't stop until she screamed out my fucking name. Her body shook, trembled, and quivered, barely being able to hold herself up. I gripped onto her thighs, carrying her up to straddle my waist, pushing her back harder into the wall.

"You want my cock? Then fucking beg for it," I demanded in a husky tone, positioning myself at her entrance.

"God, yes... please... yes..."

I pushed the tip in and rocked it back and forth. Popping it in and out, teasing her. It was the only game I loved to fucking play.

"Please…"

I forcefully pushed my dick all the way in, and she cried out in ecstasy. Immediately wrapping her arms around my neck, I gripped her ass firmer and more demanding. Making her bounce on my cock, her tits bouncing in my face. Her pants and moans ricocheted off the tiled wall.

I could feel her pussy constricting on my cock, pulsating, aching. I reached down, manipulating her clit, making her go fucking insane with need.

"Fuck yes… yes, baby…just like that. Come on my cock that belongs to you. Keep… fucking me. I'm going to come with you."

She clung to my dick as I felt her warm juices spread down my shaft. I plunged into her one last time and came just as hard.

Releasing her, getting right down to my knees so that she could squirt on my fucking face.

Claiming me.

M. Robinson

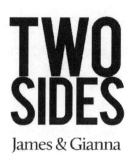

TWO SIDES

James & Gianna

CHAPTER FOUR

JAMES

I left the schoolgirl uniform on our bed and made my way back into my office, shutting the door behind me. Waiting for her. It was our anniversary, and I wanted to celebrate it *my* way. I had always been a kinky bastard, and being with Gianna only brought out the best in me.

I tried to keep busy, looking over paperwork while I waited. Failing miserably at distracting myself from my throbbing cock in my slacks. Checking my watch every few minutes, I anxiously awaited her arrival. It wouldn't be much longer now. She was due home any minute. If there was one thing Gianna knew I hated, it was to be kept waiting.

Even for her.

The sound of the garage door rumbled through the narrow hallways of our home, traveling into my office seconds later. I grinned, picturing her pretty little face when she read the note I had left taped to the interior garage door. Ordering her on what she needed to do next, knowing all she ever wanted was to appease me. Especially with my distorted fantasies, my cock ached just thinking about the game we were about to play.

I leaned back into my leather chair, rubbing my index and middle finger back and forth over my lower lip. Still tasting her from this morning. I could spend all day in between her legs, and trust me…

I fucking had.

A half-an-hour later, I heard her footsteps coming down the hallway, one right after the other. I put my glasses back on. Fixing my suit jacket and tie, looking every bit the part I was about to act. I picked up my pen and peered back down at my paperwork as the door opened, trying to hide the smile and the thrill of what was to come.

"This is so fucked up, even for you, James," Gianna chuckled, the amusement flowing through her words.

"It's Mr. Nichols, Miss Edwards," I corrected in a stern tone, glancing up over the rims of my glasses.

She smiled, cocking her head to the side. "Miss Edwards, is it?"

My greedy glare went from her black baby doll shoes to her white stockings that came up past her knees, to the short, pleated schoolgirl skirt. I just knew her pussy was bare underneath. She had suspenders holding up her skirt, and a white collared shirt that was tied in a knot high above her petite waist, showing off her toned stomach and slender hips. The first few buttons were undone, faintly exposing her bright, pink, lacy bra underneath and ample fucking cleavage fully on display. Her freshly showered hair was pulled up in pigtails with pink bows to finish off her schoolgirl attire. She smelled so fucking edible.

My cock twitched at the sight of her.

"Mr. Nichols, my teacher said you wanted to see me," she informed, breaking the silence between us. Knowing exactly the role I wanted her to play in my perverted fantasy.

I nodded to the makeshift desk I placed in front of mine, ordering her to take a seat. She placed her hands behind her back like a little girl, practically skipping her way across the room to sit down. Her skirt bouncing with each jump, allowing her perfect, luscious ass cheeks to peek out the bottom.

"Have I been a bad girl?" she asked in an innocent tone, batting her lashes at me, sensually biting her index finger once she sat down.

"On so many levels," I simply stated, leaning back in my chair again. Taking the ruler with me.

Her eyes widened, dark and dilated.

"Rumor has it, Miss Edwards, that you've been talking back to your teachers again and not following directions when ordered to do so numerous times. We've spoken about your attitude adjustment before. You got down on your knees and promised me that it would no longer be a problem," I said, slapping the ruler against the palm of my hand in a calculated rhythm, waiting for her to respond.

She bit the nail on her thumb, contemplating what she was going to say.

"What explanation do you have for yourself now, young lady?"

"Well..." She shrugged. "I'm just not very good at following orders, Mr. Nichols. I try to be a good girl, I really do, but it's just so hard," she emphasized, accentuating the last word. Giving me a devilish smile. "Besides, it's so much more fun to be the bad one," she added, spreading her legs. Proving to me that I was fucking right.

She wasn't wearing any goddamn panties.

I nodded. "I see." Allowing my eyes to roam over her perfect, pink cunt on display underneath the table, before bringing my eyes back up to meet hers. "Did you forget something this morning?"

She shook her head, acting coy. "I don't think so."

I snapped the wooden ruler hard against my desk, making her jump from the sudden smack. "Your panties, Miss Edwards."

"Oh... I thought I felt something wet. I guess I seemed to have misplaced them."

I stood, slowly rounding my desk. Leaning against the edge. Crossing one leg over the other, I pulled her panties out of the pocket of my slacks, bringing them up to my face and inhaled hard. "Hmmm..." I groaned. "Do these look familiar, Miss Edwards? I found them in my mailbox this morning. I think you wanted me to call you into my office, am I warm?"

She nodded. "More like hot."

"Do you know what happens to little girls who misbehave in school?"

"No, but I'm sure you're going to show me. Do your worst, Mr. Nichols."

"Did you just mouth off to me?"

"I—"

"Stand up," I demanded in a harsh tone. "NOW!"

She jolted again. Standing to her feet, almost knocking over her chair.

"Come to me."

She swallowed hard, stepping out in front of her desk.

"Crawl," I interrupted, and her eyes gleamed.

She slowly fell down to her knees. Her tits practically falling out of her top as she leaned forward, provocatively crawling her way to me. Only stopping when her face was inches away from my cock.

"Do you have something for me?" she purred, sitting back on her heels and looking up at me through her lashes with an expression that made my balls ache to fuck her mouth.

I crouched down to her level, immediately grabbing ahold of her face with one hand. Causing her mouth to open from the sudden grip along her cheeks. I roughly shoved her panties into her mouth, watching her fucking gag on them. I didn't hesitate, pulling her up by the hair at the nook of her neck, placing her heated body over my lap. Her torso straddled my thighs, making her ass stick straight up in the air.

"Look what we have here," I rasped, inspecting the butt plug this minx had put inside of her asshole. "You little fucking whore." I pulled the panties out from her mouth, shoving her head down onto the desk, and locking her in place. Causing her ass to stick out further in front of my face, getting her nice and ready for her fucking punishment.

"Mr. Nichols, I'm sor—"

"Count, Miss Edwards. Loud!"

She didn't oblige.

"NOW!"

She shuddered, murmuring, "One."

Whack! I slammed the wooden ruler down on her bare ass cheek, hard. Her body lurched forward.

"What part of loud did you not understand?!"

"Two!"

Whack!

"Three!"

Whack!

"Four!"

Whack, whack, whack!

"Fi...v...e!"

Whack!

And I didn't stop until her ass was bright red and fucking swollen.

Gianna

I took my punishment like the good little girl he wanted me to be. My pussy got wetter and wetter to the point it was dripping down my legs with each slap of his wrist with the ruler against my ass cheeks.

"Good girl," he praised in a husky tone I was more than familiar with when he was done.

I leaned into each and every touch as his callused fingers massaged my swollen flesh. I whimpered in pain when he made me stand at the edge of the desk, pushing my head back down onto the hardwood. Not thinking my punishment was enough. I knew better than to disobey him, he would spank my ass raw, more than he already had, like he had done countless times before.

His rough hands caressed down my back while he lowered himself down my legs, penetrating my muscles with his simple yet urgent touch. When his mouth reached my calves, he leaned forward, placing kisses down the crevice of my ass. Kneading my cheeks for a few moments, I got lost in the sensations only he could ever create within me.

He spread me open, taking hold of the small glass butt plug, twisting it inside me, pulling it in and out, fucking me with it. Taking the tip and swirling it around my opening as he placed more kisses over the rising welts from the ruler.

"Stick your tongue out, Miss Edwards. I want you to taste yourself," he whispered near my ear, placing the plug in my mouth. "Now lick it fucking clean."

I placed my lips around the warm glass, sucking it in, using my tongue to lap up all my juices. Sucking it like I would his cock, pleasing him.

"You're such a dirty little whore," he roared, lightly licking the pucker of my asshole as I continued sucking the plug in and out of my mouth. Now realizing why he wanted me freshly showered in his instructions. I tried to push myself off the cold surface, but he spanked my ass and pushed me forward yet again.

"Don't fucking move," he ordered, pinning my hips down where he wanted them.

He continued to lick from my asshole to my opening, rubbing my pussy with the palm of his hand, placing it over my clit. Tortuously making delicious circles around my bundle of nerves.

I shamelessly moaned.

What started off tender, became rough and hard. Every time I tried to rotate my hips into his hand, he slapped my sensitive ass with an open palm. Making sure that he was still the one in control.

James was always in control.

Of me.

Of him.

Of everything.

He spread my cheeks, sinking his tongue into my asshole as far as it could go, pushing in and out. Fucking my most sacred area with nothing but his warm tongue, making me go crazy with need and desire for him. He growled, loud and hard. Pushing what felt like his middle and ring fingers into my pussy, finger fucking me into submission.

I bit my lower lip when I felt his thumb probing asshole, carefully pushing it in as well. Relishing in the pain and pleasure of him spreading me open, I could feel him everywhere and all at once.

"You love that, don't you? Getting fucked in both holes," he grunted.

"Hhhhmmm... Don't stop Jam—Mr. Nicolas," I moaned, my body starting to sweat and shake all at the same time.

Wanting to come.

Needing to come.

"Fuck... you're so goddamn wet. You love being my little whore. Get that asshole nice and fucking wet to take my fucking cock."

His filthy mouth did it to me every time. My face pressed into the desk as I shook, coming so fucking hard my legs almost gave out. He didn't give me any time to recover before he was in between my legs, spreading my cheeks wider than before. Nudging the head of his cock into my asshole.

I never even heard him unzip his pants.

"Relax… let me in," he reassured in a soothing voice. "I'm almost all the way in… just relax…"

My head turned to the side, wanting to watch his face as he took me from behind.

"Just relax so I can fuck this beautiful ass. *My* beautiful ass," he groaned, spanking me.

Claiming me.

Fucking me.

He didn't stop until he was balls deep inside of me. "I'm going to fuck your asshole, Miss Edwards, and it's going to be hard and rough for being such a bad little girl."

I recognized that tone, and when he grabbed my hair by the nook of my neck and pulled back, I knew he meant every word.

"Whatever you think is right, Mr. Nichols," I purred, swaying my hips.

He thrust in and out of me, his balls slapping against my wet heat. Fucking me slowly and then more demanding, roughly gripping the locks of my hair tighter around his hand. Never letting up on taking what he wanted.

What he craved.

What was always his.

When I started to meet his thrusts, he slapped my ass not wanting me to move until he was ready. It was only a matter of time until I felt one masculine hand wrap around my throat, cutting off my air supply. I gasped, instinctively bringing my fingers up to my throat, latching onto his hand.

"Shhh… breathe," he whispered close to my ear easing up on the pressure. "That's it, baby. Breathe. You trust me. You breathe when I tell you to, understood?"

I nodded.

His grip tightened on my throat again, almost to the to the point of pain, but the pleasure he was stirring deep within my core outweighed the discomfort.

The room started to spin, coming in and out of focus, but with his cock in my ass and his hand wrapped around my throat, I couldn't help but want to come.

"Breathe." He released his grip a little, and I sucked in air.

He did this a few more times, letting me get to the edge and not allowing me to fall over. Then out of nowhere he instantly released my throat, pulled out of me, and flipped me over so fast that I never saw it coming. My back hit the desk in a loud, firm thud, bringing me back to reality. Struggling to catch my breath. Gripping onto my thighs, he spread my legs open and in one hard thrust, he was deep inside my asshole once again. Making my back arch and my mouth part, letting a scream pass my lips. He was so much deeper this way, sending me spiraling down to another intense, mind-blowing orgasm.

"So fucking tight..." he growled, slamming in and out of me. Pushing two fingers into my pussy, finger fucking my g-spot and playing with my clit at the same time.

Causing me to scream louder in ecstasy.

"Beg me to fucking come, beg me like the good little girl I want you to be."

"Please... please... Mr. Nichols, let me come..."

My whole body was shaking, and I swear you could hear my moans and screams a mile away. It didn't take long until my eyes rolled to the back of my head and my back sprung off the desk as my climax loomed, taking me under.

I came over and over again. I didn't think I would ever stop coming. He grinded into me, fucking me with passion, with love, with everything that had always been mine. He couldn't hold back any longer and released his seed deep inside of my asshole. His body immediately fell over to claim my mouth, kissing me, loving me, fucking devouring me.

"Jesus, you still always come with everything you have," he whispered in between kissing me. Looking deep into my eyes, he spoke with conviction, "Of all my loves this is the first and last. You are my sun and stars, my night, my day, my seasons, summer, winter, my sweet spring, my autumn song, the church in which I pray, my land and ocean, all that the earth can bring. Of glory and of sustenance, all that might be divine, my alpha and my omega, and all that was ever mine," he quoted Shakespeare, making me smile. Exactly like the first time we made love all those years ago.

"I love you, James."

"Happy Anniversary, baby."

He took me to bed where he made love to me all night long. Until I didn't know where he ended and I began, the way he always had.

And I always wanted.

Lucas & Alex

CHAPTER FIVE

LUCAS

I watched Alex pull her hair up off the nook of her neck as she stood at the cash register, counting the money after a long day at the restaurant. It was a hot summer night in Oak Island, North Carolina. One of the hottest we've felt in a while. My tiny little wife looked good enough to fucking eat, standing there in a yellow sundress and flip flops. Swaying her ass to "Brown Eyed Girl" playing on the old jukebox. I was supposed to be working late, needing to finish up a new remodel for the house on Barrington Drive, but I couldn't stop thinking about Half-Pint. We'd both had been working like crazy, and tourist season had only just begun for her.

It was as if she felt me, our connection stronger than fucking ever. She looked my way, catching me leaning up against the support column in the corner of the room, one leg over the other. My arms crossed over my chest, head cocked to the side, taking in every last drop of sweat that fell down her cleavage. Glistening in the light.

She gasped, placing her hand on her chest. Caught off guard to see me standing there.

Watching her.

"Oh my God, Bo! You just scared the crap out of me!" she shrieked, shaking her head. "What are you doing here? I didn't think I would see you until late tonight."

I arched an eyebrow, grinning. "Is that right?"

She narrowed her eyes at me, picking up on the slight edge in the tone of my voice.

"Where did you think you would see me, Half-Pint?" I asked, eyeing her with a predatory regard. "In bed? With my hand wrapped around my cock, stroking myself. Waiting for you."

Her eyes widened, immediately blushing. Looking around the room like we weren't alone. Even after all these years, Alex still turned bright red anytime I spoke dirty to her. Always such a goddamn lady, but I wouldn't have it any other way.

"What's gotten into you?" she breathed out, her voice shaky and unsure.

I pushed off the wall, heading toward the register, reaching her in four long strides. Causing her back to hit the adjacent wall behind the counter with a thud. Surprising her with my sudden movement. I hovered above her small frame, locking her in with my arms on each side of her face.

Leaning forward, I rasped against her lips, "You, Alex. You got into me. Ever since you were fucking born."

Her breathing hitched.

"Do you have any idea how many times I've thought about fucking you on this counter? Especially when we were kids and you started working here for your parents'. Wearing those little, thin, cotton tank tops that barely covered your tits, your tiny bikini always underneath. Just the slightest gust of wind made your nipples hard," I whispered, the backs of my fingers lightly wiping away the sweat from her chest as it raised and descended from each of my words.

"Bo..." she panted, blushing again from the needy tone in her voice.

I smiled. Nothing turned me on more than knowing I made Alex fucking wet.

For me.

"Did you think I never noticed? The way your sundresses would cling to your body after a long day of work. How they still fucking do? How about the way you would make sure that my food was always ready when I came in from surfing? Like you still do. Knowing just how much I loved it when you fed me."

She swallowed hard.

"Well, Half-Pint, I'm fucking famished. Starving in fact. For your tight, sweet little pussy. You gonna feed me? Or am I gonna have to fucking take it?"

"Bo, I—"

67

The sudden urge to make her mine was too overpowering to ignore any longer. The urge to show her over and over again just how much she belonged to me always took over.

Consuming me.

I didn't hesitate, picking her up by her ass. "Wrong fucking answer," I interrupted, setting her on the granite countertop behind the register. Her body was now perfectly proportionate with mine as I stood in between her legs.

She looked up at me with yearning and longing. The heady expression on her face was pushing me further over the edge, barely hanging onto the last bit of control I still had. I slowly reached for the hem of her dress, taking it off in one swift movement. Freeing her perky breasts within seconds, her nipples already hard, waiting for me to take them into my mouth.

I kissed my way down her neck, stopping to inhale the scent of sunscreen on her skin that always did things to me. It had since we were fucking kids. The smell of her cherry lip-gloss quickly assaulted my senses, still causing my cock to twitch as much as it did then. I continued moving down until I reached her breasts, gently biting one of her nipples into my mouth while my hand caressed and fondled the other. Her breathing escalated. Both of her soft, delicate hands made their way up my chest, gripping my hair as she gyrated her hips forward to the edge of the counter.

Her silent plea to keep going.

I continued my assault on her smooth skin, leaving a trail of desire in my wake. Kissing her lower abdomen, looking up at her with just my eyes as she was looking down at me, watching everything that I was doing with a dark, dilated, intensified gaze.

I grinned. "There's my brown-eyed girl."

She smiled, biting on her bottom lip in a sinful yet innocent way that only Alex could ever pull off.

Her hands let go of my hair to lean back for support, while my teeth latched onto the front of her silk panties. My hands went to the sides of the elastic binding, deliberately sliding them down her legs in a slow, tantalizing rhythm. Getting down on my knees as I discarded them to the side once they were past her flip-flops. Getting rid of those as well.

"You have no idea how many goddamn times I've thought about eating your pussy today, Half-Pint," I groaned, grabbing her right foot and perching it on the side of the counter as I licked my way to her core. Doing the exact same thing with the other.

I leaned back, sitting on my ankles once I was done. Needing to see her sitting there, completely spread open for me. Letting my intense gaze linger for a few seconds, admiring the fucking view of her wet, sweet, fucking pussy.

I could have come right then and there.

Fuck me...

I couldn't believe he was doing this, here, in our restaurant of all places. Thank God it was late and everyone abandoned the beach to hit the town. Prying eyes or not, he was taking me right then and there. When Lucas put his mind to something, anything… there was no telling him no.

My stubborn boy.

And I wouldn't have it any other way.

There I sat, completely open for him. Showing him every last part of me. It didn't matter that he had seen me countless times before, each time he looked at me it felt like the first.

No matter what.

I had always loved his bright blue eyes that held everything he could sometimes never say. They always spoke volumes.

Want.

Craving.

Lust.

Love.

Home.

Mine.

As if he couldn't take it any longer, he lunged forward, almost knocking me off the counter to devour me.

Licking, sucking, lapping…

Eating.

My hands tangled in his hair, clutching on for dear life while my head fell back and my eyes closed as he persisted to consume me like a starved man. It didn't take long until I was panting and moaning his name, overwhelmed by his sweet torture, coming apart.

"Fuck…" he breathed out, and our stares locked. "You taste so fucking good. I will never be able to get enough of your sweet, salty pussy. Does that feel good baby? Tell me how good."

He didn't give me a chance to answer before his tongue immediately moved to my opening, and he growled the second his tongue dipped inside, licking me clean. Making love to me with his mouth for what felt like hours, like he couldn't get enough of my heat. Making me realize he really was hungry.

For me.

He kissed his way up my body, latching onto the sides of my face. Shoving his tongue into my mouth, wanting me to savor my arousal from his lips. I heard the rustling of his pants as he let them fall down his thighs, not bothering to remove any of his clothing. His hands went around to my waist within seconds, and he effortlessly picked me up off the counter like I weighed nothing. Wrapping my legs around his waist, he was deep inside me in one hard thrust.

"Lucas!" I screamed out, unable to hold it in any longer.

We moaned in unison, taking a moment to enjoy the feeling of being connected together as one. Molding ourselves into what felt like one person. He held me tightly in his arms. Holding me against his rapidly beating heart that I knew mirrored mine.

"Christ," he growled, <u>pecking</u> my lips.

And with that, he started to shift me up and down his shaft. Thrusting into me at the same time. Engulfed in each other and the sensations of the precise angle, hitting our desired spots.

"Bo…" I panted against his lips. He never stopped kissing me.

"Look at me, baby. Let me see my brown-eyed girl," he murmured against my mouth.

I did, showing him everything he wanted. Everything he needed. How I was his and only his. How I'd always been.

He rested his forehead on mine, our eyes stayed in tune with one another. Watching what the other was giving. It took all my willpower to not let my eyes roll to the back of my head. We were both gasping and breathless for air. Our moans were getting louder and heavier, and we were both dripping with sweat. His movements were becoming faster and harder, more urgent and demanding.

My body let go, and I couldn't stop my head from falling back. Giving him the leeway to kiss and suck along my neck, stirring more emotions and sensations, coursing through my body.

"Fuck yeah… just like that, baby… come on my cock with your sweet fucking pussy that's mine…"

His filthy words were my undoing, causing me to come again. Bringing him right over the edge along with me. Both of us lost in our own thoughts and the pleasure we had just created as one.

"I fucking love you, baby," he groaned, kissing all over my face.

"I love you, too."

And he didn't stop there. He took me home and made love to me all night long.

Jacob & Lily

CHAPTER SIX

Lily

"I can't believe you got these concert tickets, Jacob! I've been wanting to see this band for years! Oh my God, I'm so excited!" I shouted in the car, unable to control my anticipation.

"It's gonna cost you, Kid."

I glanced in his direction, bringing my fingernail up to my mouth. Nervous. The last time he said it was going to cost me, I ended up on stage at Alex's restaurant doing the hokey pokey. He enjoyed the part of me putting my backside in and backside out and shaking it all about. Jacob was not the man to owe anything to, especially when he feels like he's earned it. He would make me suffer just because he found it amusing to torture me.

"Oh yeah, what do you got in mind, big man?"

He grinned, reaching over to caress my thigh. At least that's what he wanted me to think, at the last second he tried to squeeze my thigh. Knowing I was supposed to hate it but secretly loved it.

"Ohhh!" I tightly gripped his hand, holding it back as hard as I could. "Getting slow in your old age, Jacob. Gotta move faster than that!"

He chuckled, "You're still such a little shit." My strong grip was no match for his. He pushed through my grasp, squeezing the hell out of my thigh with such a force that had me thrashing around instantly.

"What was that? Huh? What about me slowing down in my old age? I'm sorry, I didn't catch that. I can't hear over your loud, whiney screaming."

"Jacob! Stop! I can't!" I surrendered, fighting him off the best I could. Even with him driving it didn't deter him. I whipped around, squealing and laughing at the same time. My legs kicking out simultaneously from the intrusion of his tickling on my over sensitive muscle.

"You what?"

"Jacob!"

"Screaming out my name isn't going to help your disposition, Kid."

"Please!"

"Begging isn't any better. If anything it's fucking worse."

"Oh my God! Fucking stop!"

"Watch your mouth," he demanded, finally stopping and pulling back his hand.

I sucked in air that wasn't available for the taking. My leg throbbing, my heart racing, trying to catch my breath. My stomach ached from laughing and screaming so damn hard.

"You almost made me pee my pants!" I tore his ball cap off the top of his head, placing it on mine instead.

Even after all these years, it still always made me feel safe.

"I hate you!" I giggled, giving him my best angry face.

"Watch it," he warned, narrowing his eyes at me. "I can turn this car around anytime. I'm the one doing you a favor, sweetheart. Like I want to stand around with a bunch of teeny fucking boppers, throwing their panties on stage to a bunch of douches who probably suck cock more than they fuck pussy."

My eyes widened, horrified. "Way to kill my fantasy!" I slapped him.

"Is that right, baby? You want to throw your panties on stage? See if one of those boys can you make you come like a man? Hate to break it to you, Kid. No one can make you come like I can. I own your pussy, have since you were a little girl... fucking throwing it at me."

My mouth dropped open, stunned by his outburst. "I did no such thing! I was always a lady! You were just a dirty old man who thought perverted things about me and my lady bits. I can't help where your deluded mind wandered."

He reached over a little, surrendering his hand in the air when I jerked back. Thinking he was coming at me to squeeze my sore thigh again. He placed his arm behind my headrest and angled his body toward me, never expecting what would come out of his mouth next.

Our eyes locked as he spoke with conviction, "You can suck my cock for that."

JACOB

My dick twitched from the filthy yet innocent way she spoke to me. There was no one in the world like my girl. Never had been.

Never would be.

"What?" she replied, caught off guard.

"You heard me. I told you it's going to cost you, now it's not only for these concert tickets but also for that saucy little fucking mouth that always seems to get you in trouble. So I'm going to shut you up with my goddamn cock." I nodded toward it. "Undo my belt and unbutton my jeans."

Her eyes dilated, shocked and turned on. It's one of the things I loved the most about her. She had this intense desire to please me, had since she was a kid, and it only got worse, or should I say better, as she got older.

"Better hurry, Lily, before I turn the car around and then you don't get to see your boys who for whatever reason you think are worth your fucking panties."

She swallowed nervously, her unsteady hands going for my buckle, waiting for the other shoe to drop. She undid them, reaching for my button next, vigorously working to free my hard cock. My dick jolted free, smacking against my stomach.

Her mouth parted, sucking in her bottom lip. Already tasting my come on her tongue. It didn't matter how many times she had sucked my cock since the first time years ago, every time seemed as if it couldn't get any better.

And each time I was proven wrong.

"Suck me, sweet girl. Fuck me with your mouth."

She grinned, loving that I was giving her control. Anytime I did she thrived on it, wanting the feeling to last as long as it could. I took the opportunity to switch over into the far lane, luckily it was dark out and there weren't many cars on the highway.

Not that it would have stopped me.

She licked her lips, leaning forward, getting up on her knees. She came to me, gently taking my cock in her hand.

"Harder, baby. Stroke me harder, make me imagine it's your tight, wet, pussy fucking my cock."

I held in a breath when she licked along the tip. Her warm lips sucking me in, inch-by-inch, her hot mouth gliding down my shaft in a slow, torturous rhythm, taking me deep and then back out.

"Christ…" I groaned, grabbing onto the back of her neck. Tugging her back down. "Fuck… baby." The sight and feel of her almost being too goddamn much. "Good girl, just like that, so good… so fucking good."

"Mmm," she hummed as she deep throated me again. Her hand moving in-sync with her mouth.

I couldn't hold back any longer, I had to touch her. I reached around her tiny frame, kneading her ass cheeks a few seconds, sliding over her panties. Needing to feel her and make her come right along with me.

"Jacob!" she squealed by surprise when she felt my fingers rub her clit.

"Don't stop. Trust me. I would never let anything happen to you," I reminded, knowing she was feeling nervous about the fact that I was still driving.

"Oh God," she hummed along my cock as I pushed my fingers into her opening. Her wetness making it easy to do so. I pumped my hips against her movements, getting lost in the way she worked me over.

Her rhythm started to match the speed of my fingers, faster… harder… deeper…

"I'm gonna come," she mumbled, coming all down the palm of my hand.

I growled and didn't give it a second thought. I pulled over onto the grass on the side of the road, threw my car into park, and pulled

79

Lily to straddle my lap. Slamming my cock so far into her pussy that she wouldn't know where I ended and she began.

Lily

I couldn't believe he was doing this. First the road head and now the quickie on the side of the road. I shouldn't be surprised, Jacob always went after what he wanted. It didn't matter the consequences, they were always damned.

I loved when he manhandled me, his dominance over me was one the hottest things any woman could ever ask for. Being married and having kids hadn't changed that, if anything it intensified.

His dick was inside of me before I even knew what was going on, what had happened. I screamed out his name, his lips crashed into mine, muffling my pleas. Making us feel like we were one person.

He didn't allow me to recover, gripping onto my hips, moving his in the opposite direction. Making me fuck him while he continued to fuck me.

"God, Jacob... what has gotten into you?"

"You, Lily. You got into me, and you've stayed there since the first time I held you in my arms. You were fucking mine," he groaned, kissing me with passion and intensity that had me coming from that alone.

My swollen clit rubbed against his lower abdomen, the head of his cock pushed right against my g-spot. It was a sensory explosion.

One right after the other.

I couldn't stop coming, and he didn't want me to.

"Fuck yes... do it... do it... don't fucking stop... don't ever fucking stop..."

I roughly grabbed the back of his neck to keep our eyes locked together. Our connection thriving all around us. You could feel it a mile away. His forehead hovered above mine as we tried to catch our breaths, trying to find our perfect rhythm.

"Don't close your eyes."

I nodded, panting profusely, his heart pounding against mine. He pushed his tongue into my eager, awaiting mouth.

"Say it," he groaned in between kissing me.

"Jacob," I breathed out, and I swear his cock got harder.

Our mouths parted and now we were both panting uncontrollably, desperately trying to cling onto every sensation of our skin on skin contact. I felt myself start to come apart yet again, and he was right there with me.

"I love you," I found myself saying before I even gave it any thought. "Jacob, Jacob, Jacob," I repeated over and over, climaxing all down his shaft and taking him right over with me. We shook from both our orgasms, passionately claiming my mouth once again.

He didn't have to say it because I already knew what he was thinking.

M. Robinson

Mine.

Dylan & Aubrey

CHAPTER SEVEN

DYLAN

"No. We need him willing and able," I said into the phone, leaning back in my office chair. Trying to get as comfortable as fucking possible, knowing I'd be here all night again. Determined to wrap up this goddamn case once and for all.

I missed my girls, especially my wife. I'd been working around the clock for the last several months, which didn't leave much time for anything else. I couldn't remember the last time I was balls deep inside Aubrey, feeling her pussy wrapped around my cock. Just the thought of it made me fucking hard.

"You still there?" Detective Sanders asked over the phone.

"Where else would I fuckin' be?"

He chuckled, "Listen, man, I know. I miss my family, too. But we all know it comes with the territory, McGraw. If anyone understands that, it's Aubrey."

"Thanks for the pep talk. You were fuckin' sayin'?"

"There has to be a reason why this guy doesn't have a record. His file should be a mile long by now. You and I both know it. We need to—" My office door abruptly opened, bringing my attention away from the voice on the phone and the paperwork in front of me, to the uninvited guest. No one barged in without knocking first, I fucking made sure of it.

I peered up, ready to give them hell for rudely interrupting. Completely caught off guard when I saw Aubrey walk over the threshold, slowly closing and locking the door behind her. She mischievously smiled with a gleam in her eyes I hadn't seen in months. Leaning her back against the door, cocking her head to the side, fucking baiting me. She knew better than to barge into my office when I was working.

Someone was being a very bad girl.

"I gotta go," I stated to Sanders who was still going on about one thing or another.

"What the fu—" I hung up.

Leaning forward, I placed my elbows on my desk, allowing my eyes to wander from her dark eyeliner to her long, thick lashes, down to the bright red lipstick on her pouty mouth. I was already imagining those lips around me, deep throating my fucking cock. My predatory regard didn't stop there. It went down to her luscious, curvy body that I could never get enough of which was now covered in a black, button-down trench coat. The belt tightly wrapped around her tiny, little waist, tied in a firm knot in the front. The hem of the coat covered just above her bright, red, fuck me heels that finished off her suspicious, but sexy as hell appearance.

"Did you forget to fuckin' knock, darlin'?" I asked, breaking the silence between us. Nodding to the door behind her.

She grinned. "Well, you see, Detective McGraw. I'm here with a real, deep, urgency. Only a man of your stature and importance could understand when a woman, such as myself, has needs," she replied in a sultry tone, pushing off the door. Provocatively placing one heeled toe in front of the other, moving to sit in one of the chairs in front of my desk.

"Is that right?" I rasped, arching an eyebrow as she slowly crossed her legs, giving me a glimpse of what she had in store. Making sure that the hem of her trench coat fell slightly open to her sides, faintly displaying the top of her lacy black thigh-highs.

When she caught me staring, she quickly closed her trench coat, not allowing me to see anything but the heavy-duty cotton material. Much to my disapproval.

"Detective," she reprimanded, dramatically placing her hand over her chest. "Why I'd never..."

"Suga', you wouldn't have come all this way wearin' thigh-highs and fuck me heels, if you didn't want me to at least look."

"I'm a lady."

"I'm a man," I simply stated.

"Now that, I do know. And what a man you are. Which is why I'm here. You see, Detective McGraw, my husband has gone missing."

"Missing, you say?"

"Yes, sir. I haven't seen him in months."

I nodded, playing along. Mostly because I wanted to see where she was going with this. "And you're just now filing a report? You can see how that seems rather suspicious?"

She theatrically sighed, shaking her head. "Do I look like a woman who could hurt her husband, Detective?" She stood, sweeping her long blonde hair over her shoulder. Gesturing to herself. "I mean, look at me. I'm a tiny little thing. You think I can overpower my big, strong, muscular husband? I mean, by all means... search me."

I stifled a laugh, holding back a smile. "In due time, Miss..."

"Ivana Fucku," she answered with a straight face, turning to sit back down.

Now, I couldn't hold back a laugh. Leaning back in my leather chair, I crossed my arms over my chest, stating, "I'm at your fuckin' service."

"I was hoping you'd say that. My husband is an extremely possessive man. It's not like him to go this long without making sure that his wife is fully satisfied in every possible way. Surely you understand, Detective. Don't you? How it would feel to go without the pleasure of his mouth and hands all over me?"

My cock twitched.

She narrowed her eyes at me with an intense stare. Her eyes bored into mine. "Which is why I've been satisfying myself for the last few months, but it's not the same." She wet her lips before biting down on the bottom one.

Eye fucking the shit out of me.

"And why is that?"

She stood again, this time provocatively striding over to me, rounding my desk. Only stopping when she was inches away from my face. The smell of her arousal was all around me as she slowly, tauntingly she sat on the edge of my desk. Running her hands seductively down her stockings, she spread her legs and placed one heeled foot on each of my thighs. I reached out wanting to touch her, but she smacked my hand out of the way, shaking her head, chastening me. A low growl escaped my throat when she began to unbutton her trench coat, one right after the other. Leaving the belt for last, never taking her eyes off mine as she provokingly unknotted that as well.

"Because, Detective," she purred, fully opening her coat. Letting it fall from her shoulders onto my desk, showing me she wasn't wearing anything but thigh-highs and heels. She leaned back onto her hands, spreading her legs even further. "No one can fuck me like my husband."

With that, she moved her hand to the side of her breast, kneading her nipples, gradually gliding her fingers down her slender, toned waist, and stopping when she reached her pink, perfect pussy. I tried to lean forward but she stopped me, pressing her heel sternly against my chest.

"Don't make me take those handcuffs and cuff you to the chair, Detective."

I put my hands up, surrendering to her.

"You promise to behave?" she questioned, knowing damn well I wouldn't.

"Always."

"My husband is also an extremely jealous man. He would have your balls if he saw the way you were looking at me," she informed, manipulating her clit from side-to-side. Causing a soft moan to escape her lips as her head rolled back.

I spoke with conviction, "Darlin', I'd gladly hand them over to fuckin' taste you, and he ain't here right now, is he? You and I both know all it would take is for me to put my hands on you, to forget all about him."

"Is that right?" she mocked, peering back up at me, cocking her head to the side and rubbing herself faster and harder. She looked right into my eyes, challenging me.

Provoking me.

"What if I only let you watch?"

And then I lost my shit.

Aubrey

There was something animalistic about the way he was staring at me. Almost like a lion before it attacks its prey, luring me with his eyes and his captivating demeanor. A sexy arrogant expression that only Dylan McGraw could ever pull off, marred his face. Even after all these years, my husband was as sexy as fucking ever. It should be a sin to look as good as he did.

With his long, blond hair tied back in a man bun. The rugged dirty blond beard on his face that already had me fantasizing about how it would feel between my legs.

I knew his cock ached just as much as my pussy throbbed.

Since he couldn't come to me, I decided I would come to him. I missed him in ways I didn't think were possible. My life had always been about Dylan. That's just the way it was, and I wouldn't have it any other way. I watched him with caution and hunger, waiting for his next move. It all happened so fast. I never saw it coming. He roughly shoved my heel out of his way, making me fall back onto his desk with a thud from the sudden shift in movement. Papers flew out beneath me.

My arms were over my head within seconds, cold metal quickly replaced the heat of his strong grasp around my wrists, followed by a loud clasping sound moments later. I leaned forward only to meet his

89

hand as it wrapped around my neck, hard. Holding me in place against his desk again.

My breathing hitched.

It was then I realized he had handcuffed me to the steel bar on the front of his desk. My eyes widened and my chest heaved, being at his mercy. Exactly how he wanted me all along. He hovered above me, needing me to understand that he was always in control.

No matter what.

Bending forward, he placed his stocky, broad, hardened frame on top of mine, making me feel so tiny beneath him. So helpless.

"You think you can come into my office and fuckin' order me around, suga'?"

"I—" He squeezed my neck harder.

"Did I say you could fuckin' talk?" he interrupted, loosening his hold.

Before I could even blink, the metal handcuffs clanked against the steel as he flipped my body over on his desk so I was laying on my stomach. My bare ass now in the air.

"You've been a very bad little girl," he whispered into my ear.

"What—" *Whack!*

I gasped, and my body jolted forward from the unexpected blow to my ass cheek.

"Dylan!" I shrieked, breaking character. Surprised by the turn of events.

"Detective McGraw," he corrected, not breaking his. Delivering another blow.

"Oh my God! I'm gonna—" *Whack!* I shuddered, rendering me silent.

"You gonna what, suga'?" he taunted close to my ear. His warm breath doing all sorts of things to me.

"You think you can be a bad girl, coming in here like a little slut, and not be punished? What kind of Detective do you think I am? Who do you think you're fuckin' with, darlin'?"

"Dylan, I mean it! You better—" *Whack!* "Oh my God! I'm not going to be able to sit for a week! Stop!"

"Shhh! Or I'll gag you."

My eyes widened as I placed my face onto the desk to look at him. "You wouldn't."

"Fuckin' try me."

I couldn't believe he was being this way with me. *Who was this man? What the hell just happened?*

"I could look past the way you were barkin' orders at me. I could even let go of the fact that you barged into my office uninvited. But what I can't excuse is how you got into your car, drove across town, and walked through my place of fuckin' employment... where there's nothing but horny ass men that are pussy deprived... fuckin' naked. I'm doing your husband a fuckin' favor."

Whack, whack, whack.

Shit.

"Nobody saw me. I made sure of it," I explained, trying to catch my breath. I knew the risk I was taking, showing up to his office naked. How he may react as soon as he discovered my little surprise.

I whimpered when I felt his hand on my ass again, except this time he was gently rubbing the red, swollen cheeks in comfort.

"I love you. I'm yours," I added, hoping he would take pity and finally give me what I came for in the first place.

I heard him undoing his belt, unzipped his pants and letting them fall to the floor. In one swift, sudden movement, he turned me back over and pulled me to the edge of the desk by my thighs. Ignoring the crumbling paper beneath me. Angling my pussy right in front of his hard cock. I rocked my hips, wanting to feel him any way I could.

"You think I should give you what you obviously came for, darlin'?" he teased, kissing his way from my ankle to my thigh, inch-by-inch. Making me squirm from the warm wake of his tongue.

I nodded, giving him the best doe-eyed expression I could muster. Once he got to where we both wanted him, he inhaled the scent of my pussy. Rubbing his nose up and down my swollen clit as I watched with hooded eyes. Swallowing hard, my mouth parted.

He kissed my nub, slowly sucking it in between his lips. The light suction slowly pulled back the hood of my clit, and he placed my heels on the edge of his desk, giving him more range to assault my sacred area.

I could have come from that alone.

His tongue slid down to my opening. "You want me to fuck you with my mouth, suga'?"

I fervently nodded. Ready to beg if I had to.

"Say it! Tell me what you fuckin' want," he ordered in a husky tone. Nudging his nose on my clit again, sending me into a frenzy. I wanted to thread my hands through his hair.

"Please..." I shamelessly pleaded.

"Please, what?"

"Please fuck me with your mouth."

He growled, loud and hard. Shoving his tongue as deep as it would go into my heat, causing my juices to flow loosely. Letting him savor every last drop.

"You have the sweetest goddamn taste," he groaned, licking, sucking, devouring me.

Sucking on my clit harder and more demanding, moving his head up and down and in a side-to-side motion. Making me squirm and quiver all at once. Struggling against the cuffs, I yearned to grab ahold of him as he fucked me with his tongue. He continued to rub his face all around my pussy, unable to get enough of me. Wanting my wetness all over him, not just around his mouth.

"Beg me. Beg me to fuckin' come like a good little girl," he ordered, never letting up on the fucking torture.

"Please, babe, please... make me come..."

His rough, callused hands glided up to my breasts. He roughly kneaded my mounds, pulling at my nipples and making me come

93

apart. It had been so long since he'd touched me like that. Pushing his middle and ring fingers deep inside me next, aiming them directly to my g-spot. He ate my pussy exactly how I wanted him to, exactly how I'd been fantasizing about on all those late nights alone in bed without him. I started to move my hips, fucking his face the way he wanted me to.

The way he loved.

"Please... please... please..." I brazenly pleaded some more.

I heard him chuckling while he lapped at my bundle of nerves, manipulating them and sucking them in a way that had me panting and breaking to pieces in front of him. His fingers moved faster and became more urgent. My pussy clamped down, letting him know I was close. He rotated his head and moved faster, much more insistent until I couldn't hold back any longer and screamed out his name.

He didn't give me any chance to recover. He fucked me with his mouth, tongue, and fingers, over and over again, till I just kept coming, my juices running down his face, chin, and neck. Exactly how he wanted me to. Relishing in the sensations his beard alone was inflicting on my pussy.

The second his lips touched mine, he growled and opened them. His tongue plunged deep inside my mouth and I moaned, tasting myself all over his lips.

"You taste so fuckin' good, darlin'. I will never get enough of your sweet pussy. I was starving for you," he rasped into my awaiting mouth.

"Detective McGraw," I managed to moan, making him grin.

His hands were all over me, roaming, feeling every curve like he couldn't decide where he wanted to touch me the most. I leaned into every touch and sensation, needing to feel him like I needed air to breathe.

I couldn't get enough of him.

He slammed his cock inside of me, jarring my body toward the head of his desk from the hard thrust. The handcuffs pinched at my wrists, causing them to sting and burn as he roughly took what he wanted.

Me.

Slamming in and out of me, each thrust more demanding than the last. He fucked me like he wanted to make us one person, in a way he hadn't in months. Nothing compared to the way Dylan was with me.

Not one damn thing.

"Right there… don't stop… right there…" I eagerly panted when he moved my legs to the side of his body, grabbing onto my hips for leverage as he pounded into me. His cock hitting my g-spot from that angle.

"Here. Right here, baby," he groaned, moving his hips in the opposite direction. "Your pussy is so fuckin' tight, so fuckin' wet, so fuckin' good…"

My eyes rolled to the back of my head as my back arched off the desk, coming so hard that I saw stars. Dylan's mouth stifled my screams of ecstasy.

He unlocked my handcuffs, picked me up under my arms, and wrapped my already shaky legs around his waist. His hands gripped onto my ass, spinning us around until my back hit the door so fast that it should have surprised me, but it didn't. It only intensified my desire and need for him. He slammed into my wet pussy once again, sending me over the edge. His dick had me scratching at his back, unable to get enough. He thrust in and out of me, hitting my g-spot with every push and pull. It wasn't nice or soft. It was pure, unadulterated abandonment.

We were fucking.

I was close to release within minutes. He thrust deep into the back of my pussy and just started to move his hips, guiding me up and down his dick. His lower abdomen glided on my clit, and I threw my head back against the wall matching his hip movement.

I came hard.

His hips jerked forward, and his hand covered my overly enthused mouth, making me whimper. Releasing my mouth, he placed one of his hands around my throat and his other on my hip, gripping hard. Applying ample pressure to both. He forcefully and

Austin & Briggs

CHAPTER EIGHT

AUSTIN

"Momma! Momma! Momma! Did you see? Did you see how fast I ran?" Amari shouted, running up to us on the Brooklyn Bridge.

"I did! Of course, I did!" Briggs exclaimed, picking her up. Throwing her legs around her waist and holding her tight against her chest.

"Momma, when we gonna to see my unkey?"

"Baby girl, remember we told you, Unkey doesn't live here anymore, and you can no longer call him your unkey," Briggs answered for the tenth time, Amari kept asking about her Uncle Martinez.

Amari scratched the back of her head, confused. "I know, but he my unkey."

I laughed. We couldn't argue with that. "Come here," I ordered, taking her out of Briggs' arms. "You're too smart for your own good."

"I know. I'm a good girl. Unkey says I am."

Now it was Briggs' turn to laugh, kissing the side of Amari's face. I never got tired of watching her hold our kids. The babies that she gave me were the loves of my life.

Aside from *her*.

"Amari! You run too fast for me. I'm not going to be able to catch up with you soon," Sarah, our nanny, said panting, out of breath. Running up to us, pulling me away from my thoughts.

We had three kids, so I decided to hire a nanny a few months after our last was born, wanting to surprise Briggs. She didn't appreciate the gesture at first, saying she didn't feel comfortable with it. She changed her tune after having Sarah's help for a few weeks, admitting that she was a Godsend. She'd been with us almost a year and a half now.

"I'll take her," Sarah insisted, pulling her out of my arms. "You two go enjoy your time together. I'll take the kids back to the hotel for some swimming." She peered down at our crew. "Let's go, minions, let mommy and daddy relax for a little while." Shooting us one last smile before she turned, leaving with our babies.

"We will be back to tuck you in," Briggs called out behind them. Amari turned around, smiling wide and nodding.

We stood there and waved until they disappeared into the crowd of tourists that were also exiting the bridge.

"So, it's just you and me. What shall we do?" Briggs turned to me, wrapping her arms around my waist. Looking up to my face, batting her lashes.

"Well, I can think of a few things," I confessed, with a shit-eating grin on my face. "All involve public indecency and possible jail time, but I'd gladly do the time for the crime just to see your face when I'm balls deep inside you on the edge of the bridge."

She slapped my chest, giving me a little shove. Giggling. Little did she know I wasn't joking. We were here to celebrate me being sober and drug-free for seven fucking years. I had come full circle in my life since Briggs brought me here all those years ago. I could still hear her telling me to jump, to end my life because I was killing myself anyway with all the drugs. Taking her right along with me.

When I closed my eyes, I relived that day over and over again. A daily reminder of why I had to stay clean. Of what I could lose if I didn't. The consequences I didn't ever want to endure again.

I barely survived it the first time.

I wouldn't live through it the second.

So, here we were standing in the exact same spot on the Brooklyn Bridge that opened my drug-hazed eyes once upon a time. For what seemed like a long fucking time ago.

"Austin, I'm calling bullshit. I don't think you have the bal—" Before she could insult my manhood, I backed her into the cement wall, right underneath the arch that looked like angel wings. Caging her in with my strong arms.

Getting right up into her face.

"Do you think this is bullshit?" My mouth collided with hers, our tongues doing a sinful dance as I reached my hand down to her thigh. "How about this?" I slowly moved my palm up her long, sexy as fuck legs, under her black skirt, and right to the seam of her lacey panties. Causing her to gasp in surprise when I started to rub her already moistened pussy through the fabric. She wouldn't openly admit it, but I knew what we were doing excited her in a way she never thought possible.

"Stop! People are staring."

"What people?" I groaned against her mouth, sucking her bottom lip between my teeth.

I only ever had eyes for her.

"That little old couple, Austin. You're going to give that man a heart attack." She tried to shove me off, but I didn't budge. Pulling her panties to the side, finding her clit. Her head fell back against the wall as soon as I started to work her over, a soft moan betraying her adamant refusals.

"Fuck them. I want to fuck you. Right here, right fucking now."

I didn't let up on the sweet torture of her pussy, flicking her clit like I knew she loved. There wasn't many people left on the bridge as the sun started to set over the Hudson River. I released her lips, causing her to whimper from the loss. Looking around to make sure no one was in viewing distance, I quickly fell to my knees in front of her. Forcefully gripping onto her thigh and lifting it so her black combat boot was now resting on the railing to her right but still hidden in the shadows of the arch. My head ducked under her skirt, and my tongue immediately found her folds, licking her bare pussy from her opening to her clit. Pulling her hood back with my teeth, sucking her nub into my heated mouth, showing her just how much I wasn't bullshitting.

Her body squirmed, trembled, and rocked with each stroke of my tongue. I knew she was close, I could hear her stifling her screams.

"Yes...yes...yes..." she whispered, trying to control her erratic breathing.

"I put you through Hell here. Now I'm going to show you Heaven with my cock," I said loud enough for her to hear.

"Austin... Austin..."

"That's right, you little minx, say my name."

"No... No... People, people are coming." She barely got the words out, tapping on my head.

I peeked out, coming face to face with a tour group. Whispering to each other, pointing fingers at us like we were some sort of bridge act.

"Nothing to see here, folks. Just tying my wife's shoes." I looked up at Briggs, grinning, grabbing the laces of her boot and pretending to tie them.

Fuck that was a close one.

103

Briggs

Once Austin set his mind to something, he did it. No matter the consequence. In this case, I predicted we'd have to call Sarah and have her bail us out of jail for fucking in public. I wasn't going to lie, I got a certain thrill knowing at any second we could get caught, but I didn't let Austin in on that little secret. Instead, I let him have his way with me on the side of the fucking Brooklyn Bridge like we were two teenagers in heat.

"I'm not done with you yet, Daisy." He stood, pulling me into his chest with a thud. "Neither is my pierced fucking cock."

With that, he bent down, picking me up by my thighs. Wrapping my legs around his waist, the cool night breeze grazed my ass cheeks that were peaking out the bottom of my skirt. The buckle of his jeans rubbed me in all the right places as he carried me over to the wrought-iron bench a few strides away. I rocked my hips into his hard shaft that was now bulging in his pants, relishing in the rough exterior. He brought his lips up to my neck, licking, nipping and blowing, sucking my earlobe between his teeth. Letting out an animalistic groan the faster my movements became.

"I'm going to make you come so fucking hard, you won't remember where you are."

"Ahhhh… is that a challenge?" I breathed out, my head rolled back as I continued to dry-fuck his dick.

"No, sweetheart, that's a fucking promise."

One minute I was wrapped around him, and the next I was straddling his thighs backward, with my knees on the bench as he fumbled to free his cock. I leaned forward, digging my nails into his muscular thighs, opening myself up wide for him. Looking over my shoulder with nothing but mischief and need in my eyes, waiting for his next move.

His hands reached forward gripping my curves and slamming my eager pussy down on his cock. Stilling once he was balls deep, letting me get acclimated to his size.

Austin's dick was as huge as his fucking heart.

"I swear to God, I will never grow tired of your fucking massive cock," I moaned, his piercing hitting me exactly where I wanted it to.

I could feel him smiling behind me. "Massive, huh?"

Throwing caution to the wind, I began to sway my hips, doing a sultry dance to the music playing in my head. Taking me back to the night in Miami, the night I met him. Moving my body in a similar motion, fucking him just the way he liked. Being here in the now with the man of my fucking dreams.

My husband.

Taking ahold of my hips once again, he guided my slick pussy up and down his shaft, starting slow but quickly picking up the pace. We didn't have much time, voices sounding in the distance over the slapping of our now sweaty bodies.

"Squeeze my fucking cock. Just like that, baby. Ride me faster, harder. Fucking fuck me."

He slapped my ass once, then twice. Suddenly gripping my throat, bringing my back to his chest. Holding me in place by my chin, using his other hand to manipulate my clit as I rode him reversed cowgirl style on the bench. My knees began to sting from the friction, but I ignored the pain, backing my ass up even further, giving him a different angle.

He growled in appreciation, pounding into me even harder.

"Right there, babe. Yes... faster, faster, faster," I screamed, not caring who the fuck heard me now. Austin's strong hand came up over my lips, muffling my screams as I came full force on his dick, my come dripping down between us.

"Fuck!" he growled, biting my shoulder. Emptying every last bit of his seed into me core.

We sat there panting, exhausted from our little escapade as another tour group approached. Thanking God that is was dark now and we blended into the shadows.

"Do you know why I brought you here today?" he questioned, breaking the silence, lifting me up and placing sideways in his lap.

"Besides to do naughty deeds in public." We both laughed.

"It has been seven years since I last got high, Briggs. Seven fucking years. I wanted to bring you here to celebrate and make new memories to replace the bad ones that were still here," he paused to let his words sink in. "For the both of us."

"I'm so proud of you. I couldn't ask for a better husband or father for our kids, Austin."

"I almost died here. And all I want to do is live... for you. Our kids. Our family."

"That's all I ever want to hear."

We spent the next few hours making new memories all over New York.

And we didn't get caught.

𝕰𝖑 𝕯𝖎𝖆𝖇𝖑𝖔

Martinez & Lexi

CHAPTER NINE

MARTINEZ

"You scared?" I asked, sliding Lexi's hair to the side of her neck. Placing soft kisses along her shoulder blades as I sat behind her in the limo.

Her body was facing toward the black tinted window, her eyes glued to the scene in front of her. All of The Madam's guests dressed in costume only, walking up to The Cathouse in the sinful city of Miami.

She shook her head no, glancing back at me with a crooked smile. "I trust you."

I grinned, putting on the full-faced, red mask, with my dark black hair slicked back. I needed to remain unrecognizable, a fucking shadow in the night.

Lexi gasped at the sight of me, taking in my appearance as I cocked my head to the side. Letting out a devilish groan from deep in my chest, causing her cheeks to flush. I was wearing my signature black button-down collared shirt, a black Armani suit, and black leather gloves. A devil's mask completed my New Year's Eve Masquerade ensemble.

Evil never looked so fucking good.

I leaned over her lap, opening the door beside her. Grabbing her hand at the last second, stepping out first and bringing her right along with me. She quickly followed close behind, instantly taking in all her surroundings.

It was New Year's Eve and I wanted to fucking celebrate. It was time that El Diablo came out to fucking play, except this time…

I would be taking Lexi to Hell right along with me. My inferno wasn't always so bad. In fact, it would be quite fucking enticing. Which Lexi would learn soon enough tonight.

Besides, lust had always been my favorite fucking sin and that hadn't changed just because I *died*.

I turned around, slowly licking my lips. Watching Lexi who I purposely dressed like a goddamn angel.

The irony was not lost on her.

But I didn't want it to be.

She wore a white lace corset that had her ample tits busting at the seams, just ready for the taking. It came up to her ribs, accentuating her slender waist and luscious fucking thighs. A silver chain garter belt held up white thigh-highs, her panties perfectly placed, hardly covering her ass and pussy. Fuck me heels finished off her barely there ensemble. Her long, dark hair flowed loosely down her back, and she wore a glittery, solid white mask that covered just her eyes.

"Cariño, look me in the eyes," I demanded in a harsh tone she was more than familiar with.

She did.

"You don't leave my side, understood?"

She eyed me warily but nodded. "Where are we, Alejandro?"

"You don't get to ask questions either. We're where I want us to be, that's the only answer you'll get tonight." My gaze immediately fell to her parted lips, she was surprised by my response. "You can be scared, Lexi. In all honesty, I fucking want you to be."

With that, I turned around, once again leading the way. We walked through the front wrought-iron doors that led into the mansion, and it was exactly the way I remembered it.

I hadn't been there in decades.

It still had the same aura and magnetic pull about it. The smell of pussy and sex was all around us. Almost suffocating you with the need to want to fuck. There was translucent lighting everywhere. Half naked women dancing on poles that were set up in several places around the open room, food laid on the bare skin of women and men, and waitresses walking around topless wearing nothing but G-strings. But everyone was wearing a mask, so you couldn't see their faces.

Which only made it all the more goddamn alluring.

"Martinez," the Madam called out, bringing my attention to her before I could catch Lexi's reaction to the seediness before her. I shouldn't have been surprised that she recognized me. She could always pick a face out of any crowd.

Even a masked one.

I sneered, glaring in her direction. She cunningly smiled. "Oh yes, my apologies. What are they calling you these days?"

"A fucking pussy," Mika interrupted, stepping up beside Lilith. "Word around the streets is someone's stepped into your Armani dress shoes, motherfucker. How's it feel to be replaced, you old fuck?"

I didn't say a word, I didn't even move. I knew exactly whom this hijo de puta was talking about, and the culprit hadn't just stepped into my shoes, he'd been on the scene for decades. Hiding behind the only thing that let him get away with murder.

The law.

Unlike me, he wasn't born into that way of life, but that didn't stop him from wanting it nonetheless.

"El Santo, right?" Mika chimed in with his name. You and you're spic friends, always come up with villain names."

I didn't talk about Damian. The man, many called El Santo. Not because I was fucking afraid of him, I feared no one.

But evil didn't always hide in the shadows, in the darkness like I did. Most of the time, it was out in the open, in fucking plain sight by a man you'd least expect.

111

Who everyone thought…

Was an angel here on earth.

"Here's a little piece of advice. I wouldn't talk about things you don't know, Mika. Might come back and fuck you in the ass like I did your girl, here." I nodded to Lilith, feeling Lexi's intense stare burning holes on the side of my face.

"Speaking about taking it up the ass, who's this pretty, little thing?" He stepped toward Lexi, offering her his hand, but I stepped in between them, placing her securely behind me. Giving him a menacing glare, I resisted the urge to knock him the fuck out for even looking in her direction, but the last thing I needed was to make a scene.

I wasn't even supposed to be there.

"Look at her again, hijo de puta, and it'll be the last thing you'll fucking look at," I warned, getting right up to his face.

"Mika…" the Madam coaxed, grabbing his arm.

His jaw clenched. "Someone doesn't know how to share his toys. Who would have thought?" He stepped back, placing his hands up in the air in a surrendering gesture.

Mocking me.

Lilith peered intently at Lexi, trying to act like she wasn't caught off guard by my possessiveness over a woman. In all the years she'd known me, she never once saw that happen.

"Welcome to The Cathouse, darling," she added. "Martinez, take her to explore. It's why you came here tonight, right? To have some fun. The kind you know only I could provide? Just remember one thing, don't do anything I wouldn't do... at least twice." She eyed Lexi one last time and left.

I knew Lexi had thousands of questions running through her head, but that's not what tonight was about. I'd answer them all at another time. Or on second thought, I probably wouldn't.

I grabbed onto her hand again, making my way up one of the elegant stairways. Music vibrated the speakers throughout the entire mansion. The Madam wanted to make you think she was just setting up the scene, the mood, when in reality she was trying to drown out the screams.

"Alejandro," Lexi murmured loud enough for me to hear, gripping onto my hand tighter. Locking her arm around mine, needing to feel more secure.

I couldn't help but chuckle, she was so fucking cute when she was nervous. I guided her into one of the rooms that used to be one of my favorites.

Lexi gasped, jerking back when she crossed the threshold.

VIPs were everywhere.

Some were straddling men, others were going at it with women, and some were even in groups, taking it in every fucking hole. She watched as they sucked cock and ate pussy. Being fucked and receiving pleasure. Her eyes couldn't focus on one thing for very long. Her mouth hung open.

Not that I could blame her.

I walked around, stopping once I was standing behind her. Tugging her hair away from her neck, breathing in her vanilla scent.

I reassured, "No one touches you but me, Cariño."

"And you? No one is touching you, right?" she asked, slightly angling her head to look at me.

"I just want to watch. You know how much I love to fucking watch."

Lexi

I had so many questions, and not nearly enough answers.

My eyes went back to the scenes unfolding in front of me as we walked through the rooms, one by one. Each one different than the last, the only thing they had in common was the heady, blatant fucking.

One of the back rooms caught my attention in particular, and the crazy thing about was, Martinez sensed it.

"It's like it's calling your name," he simply stated, looking at me. "Go on, Lexi. Show me the way."

I swallowed hard, cautiously stepping out in front of him. Slowly moving in the direction of the room, something about its allure was pulling me to it. Something I had no control over, no power. I couldn't have walked away even if I wanted to.

And I didn't want to.

As soon as I opened the door, the clock struck midnight, sounding throughout the mansion, and the lights immediately shut off. I couldn't see a foot in front of me. One would think that the guests would experience paranoia and panic, it was the exact opposite…

Everyone was just waiting.

Especially me.

The music changed and I recognized it, "Moonlight Sonata by Beethoven echoed off the walls. I had danced my ballet to it millions of times. It was one of my favorite melodies to rehearse to.

I heard the door close behind me. Martinez grabbed me around the waist as he leaned against the wood frame. Holding me tight against his hard cock that he didn't even try to hide.

As if on cue, soft light illuminated around the open room, candles suddenly lit, spreading throughout the entire space as if they magically appeared out of thin air. I didn't even see anyone light them. It gave the large area a translucent appearance. Excitement began to course through me, making me wonder what was next.

From the four corners of the room, women all dressed in nothing but heels were present. They all took center stage like I had done countless times during performances. I couldn't take my eyes off them, they were so beautiful, so flawless, and I didn't think women like that even existed.

They were perfection in every form of the word.

Their hips swayed to the beat of the music. I didn't have to see the guests faces to know that they were all aroused, which was exactly the point. They started to dance provocatively, seducing everyone in the room.

Including me.

Each one of their movements was carnal and sinful. I watched with a hooded glare as the women captivated the attention of every last person in the room. They were made for sex. I was hypnotized by the allure of it all.

My panties became soaking wet.

The women moved their way toward one another, dancing on each other. Kissing, tasting, feeling each other, the sensations from the people in the room only enticed them to keep going.

I saw men start to pull out their hard cocks, stroking themselves to the visions of the pussy in front of them. It didn't stop there. More women came into the room, dressed exactly the same, encouraging the guests to touch them, play with them, feeling every last inch of their hard bodies.

I surveyed the room, breathing in the smell of lust, abandonment, and pussy.

Martinez's hands eased their way up my thighs. His fingers caressed and kneaded at my already sensitive skin, as Beethoven's melody continued to assault my senses. Mimicking his hands on my body.

He rubbed his nose along the back and sides of my neck. Rasping into my ear, "I don't even have to touch you to know that you're soaking fucking wet."

His hand roamed to my pussy anyway. I couldn't resist the urge to moan when his fingers found the layer of silk right above my clit. The palm of his hand swayed back and forth on my pussy to the melody of the music. I could feel my moisture starting to seep through the thin fabric as his other hand slowly moved its way up my body. I leaned into his touch, his fingers igniting something familiar deep within. I didn't know where I wanted him to touch me the most.

My whole body was on fire.

"I don't know whether to fuck you or spank you for being this wet. Is it for me or them, Cariño?"

"Both," I honestly replied, swaying my ass against his cock. Silently pleading for him to fuck me.

He didn't touch me where I wanted him the most. Instead, he teased my pussy on top of my panties, his other hand pulling down the front of my corset, freeing my breasts.

I should have stopped him.

I should have told him no.

I didn't.

I wanted him to caress me. I wanted to feel like I was his. I wanted him to take me in this room, claim me in front of these strangers that I would never see again.

I wanted all that and more.

I bit my bottom lip as I watched a man get sucked off by a woman, who was sitting on another man's face. Getting fucking devoured.

Her head fell back, as did mine. Martinez finally pushed two fingers inside of me with no warning. He wasn't soft or gentle. My eyes closed on their own as he pushed harder on my g-spot.

"You close your eyes again, and I'll fucking stop. I brought you here to watch, and I expect nothing less," he ordered, kissing and sucking on my neck.

I whimpered when he bit me, opening my heavy eyes.

"Good girl," he whispered in my ear, sucking on my earlobe.

"Mmmm…" I moaned so close to coming from the sweet torture that only his callused fingers could produce. The bastard knew it, too.

I leaned into his ear and blatantly admitted, "Please, Alejandro. Please just give me what I want."

"Here? In front of all these people?"

"Strangers," I corrected.

"Is that what you want? To be fucked in a room full of strangers, Lexi?"

"Yes…"

He chuckled, "Good girl," he praised again, groaning.

I could feel his teeth as he nibbled my flesh, making me feel both pleasure and pain. I grabbed the back of his head, pulling him and molding him into me as his hand went to his slacks, pulling down his zipper. I could hear panting all around me from the endless amounts of skin on skin contact, but I didn't care.

I was too far gone.

Martinez grabbed my chin, turning my face to meet his lips. Urgently kissing me, our tongues twirling, as we tasted each other for what seemed like the first time ever. He sucked on my bottom lip as he pulled out his cock, finally fucking freeing it. He rubbed the head of his dick along my slit, getting it nice and wet, circling my clit, and preparing for his grand entrance. But he didn't slam into me like I assumed he would. He finger fucked me with his pre-come, mixing both our juices together.

As if he was marking me.

Pissing on his territory like a rabid dog.

He roughly placed my body where he wanted me. Pushing his cock inside my opening in one solid thrust, balls deep. I shuddered.

Instantly coming on his cock.

"Fuck… you feel good. I've been thinking about this pussy all day."

We stayed like that for several seconds just enjoying the feel of one another. Until he wrapped his hand around my neck and squeezed lightly as he started to thrust in and out of me. Locking me in place, holding me in front of him, not allowing me to move an inch.

He was completely in control.

119

Exactly how I wanted him to be.

"Harder... fuck me harder," I begged as he gripped onto my waist with such force that I knew it would leave bruises.

The harder he fucked me, the tighter I squeezed on his shaft. I could feel my come dripping down my ass, onto his balls, and down our legs. I met him with each and every thrust until I couldn't take it anymore and came so fucking hard, my legs gave out.

Martinez caught me before I fell to the ground, straddling my legs around his waist. He was far from done with me yet. He slammed my back against the door, causing me to see stars from the impact. He didn't let up, he fucked me harder, growling, cursing, and saying filthy things in Spanish in my ear.

As I watched the fucking show unfolding in front of me.

"Christ..." he groaned out, thrusting inside me one last time before emptying his seed as far as it could go.

My eyes widened as he shoved his tongue into my mouth, eating me alive. Devouring my face.

"I'm not on any birth control," I said in between kisses.

He grinned against my lips, resting his forehead over mine and rasped, "I know." Kissing me one last time before adding, "Happy fucking New Year, Cariño."

Creed & Mia

CHAPTER TEN

CREED

"Not gonna say it again, Pippin. You're up to no good, yeah?" I asked, driving her Jeep back toward my house.

"No," she sternly stated, looking in my direction from the passenger seat.

"Think you can lie to me? Think I wouldn't have fuckin' found out? Walk me through your thought process, princess... please, fuckin' enlighten me."

"I'm not talking to you when you're like this," she replied, shaking her head. Crossing her arms over her chest, causing me to give her a side-glance.

Fuck, her tits were huge.

I turned my eyes back on the road, remembering how pissed I was at her.

121

"There's no point in bringing it up, either. It's not like it was this huge discussion, he just mentioned it in passing. That's all. You're letting your mind run wild like you always do, Creed."

"The only place my mind is runnin' is to those tits of yours, sweetheart."

She quickly peered out the window, trying to hide her smile.

"Not gonna ask again, Mia. Did you think I wouldn't have found out?"

She sighed, knowing I wasn't going to let up until I got a straight answer.

"I was hoping you wouldn't, but I should have known better. You seem to find out everything at any cost."

"Don't you ever fuckin' forget it either." I grinned. "Noah's lucky he's my goddamn blood, or I woulda had put him to ground already, for the way—"

"Oh my God, Creed! Must you solve everything with violence? Can't you just use your words? You know, words… those things that come out of your mouth? They usually have a few syllables attached to them? I swear you're like a barbarian, just grunting commands left and right. You'd be surprised how effective just talking could be if you actually gave it a try sometime."

"And yet here we are havin' what I thought was a fuckin' conversation."

"Oh." She turned to look at me, arching an eyebrow. "I thought this was just you barking more orders. Surely, you see how I could confuse the two, yeah?" she mocked in a condescending tone I didn't fucking appreciate.

"Only thing that seems to come out of my mouth these days is my tongue on your pussy, but ain't ever heard you complain about that, anyway."

She jerked back, her eyes widened.

"Ya feel me?" I patronized, slowly moving my hand up her inner thigh after I parked her Jeep in my driveway. "Don't got anythin' to sass at me about now, do you? Not when my hand is this close to your pussy."

She swallowed hard, waiting for my next move.

"Yeah... that's what I fuckin' thought," I added, swinging the door open and getting out of the Jeep. Leaving her there, craving my touch.

If there was anything I'd learned in the last month and a half since I found out she was pregnant, it was how fucking wet and horny it made her. Baby girl was insatiable, not that I was fucking complaining. I loved working her over, especially knowing the fact that I was ruining her for any other man.

Not that she was going anywhere.

She was fucking mine.

End of story.

I had been home on and off over the last few weeks. Pops had me on the road again, making sure everything continued to run smoothly. Which meant I hadn't spent much time with her either, making it that much easier for my little shit of a brother to try to piss on my territory. Planting thoughts in Mia's head that maybe they should move in together after the baby was born, so he could be there for her at all hours of the day and night.

I needed to shut that shit down real fucking quick. Ain't gonna happen.

I walked into the garage to grab my tools, needing to get rid of the violent thoughts. Wanting to hurt him for even thinking about Mia in any way, other than his baby mama. Trying to stay focused on the task at hand of putting new tires on my bike. Riding around across the state was starting to take a toll on my old girl.

I made my way back out from the garage, trying to shake off the thoughts of the two of them being together. Only to find Mia pulling the air compressor I took from the clubhouse out from the back of her Jeep.

"The fuck?" I roared, my temper once again looming. Dropping my tools, I was over to her in three strides, each step more determined than the last. Roughly pulling the compressor out of her hands.

"Ouch! What was that for?" she bit back, trying to pull it out of my strong grasp.

"You're pregnant!"

"Thank you, Captain Obvious! Stop!" she demanded, swatting my arms away. "I'm trying to help you."

"Does it look like I need your fuckin' help?"

"Why are you being such an asshole? Let me help, you stubborn man!" She continued to wrestle with me, but I wasn't going to ease up.

Fuck that.

"Pippin, if I needed your help then we would have much bigger problems, ya feel me? Now sit your pretty little ass down and let me handle my business."

"Ugh! Stop ordering me around! I'm pregnant! Not an invalid! Let me—"

"The only thing I'm gonna let you do, is titty fuck me once I'm done here."

She shoved me as hard as she could, but I barely wavered. Pissing her off even more.

Damn fucking hormones.

"Stop being so vulgar! And stop bossing me around! I'm your girlfriend, not your child!"

I didn't hesitate, placing the compressor on the gravel and getting right up in her face. "No, sweetheart, you're my old lady. Who's bein' a pain in my fuckin' ass." Leaning over, I abruptly picked her up. Avoiding her midsection, throwing her over my shoulder as if she weighed nothing. Not fazed by her weak ass attempts to fight me off.

"Stop manhandling me!"

"Stop fussin' like you don't want me to. We both know how wet this is makin' your silk fuckin' panties," I mocked, walking into the house, smacking her ass for good measure.

"You arrogant dick!" She pounded on my back as I carried her through the hallway down to my bedroom, kicking the door shut behind me.

"No shit, Mia. It's one of my best qualities." I carefully slammed her ass onto the soft mattress, removing my cut. She immediately turned around, trying to crawl away from me, causing me to chuckle.

I grabbed her ankle, tugging her back toward me. Making her squeal. "Babe, if I want in. I'm gettin' in," I rasped, flipping her over in one quick, sudden motion.

Kneeling on the bed, I hovered above her, locking her arms above her head. Holding her in place, I peered deep into her eyes and spoke with conviction, "This is how it's gonna go down. I'm gonna angry fuck you now, and then you're gonna beg me to make you come with that saucy, little mouth that never seems to know when to shut the fuck up. Yeah?"

"You wouldn't dare," I offered in a shaky voice, mostly because I wanted everything he just said.

"Try me."

I smiled, cocking my head to the side, provoking him even more. "I'm sorry, but visiting hours are over. I'm afraid you will have to come back later when you can be a gentleman."

He grinned, arching an eyebrow. Getting closer to my face, he started to kiss his way from the corner of my lips, down to my chin and neck. Working his way toward my breasts that were just as eager for his touch.

"Oh, I will be comin', question is... will I let you."

I inadvertently moaned. I couldn't help it. This man not only pissed me off every chance he got, but he also made me hot as hell. Needing him so damn bad. I couldn't fathom how I could go from one extreme to the other within seconds.

"You nervous, Mia?"

"Yes..."

"Why?"

"Because it's you."

"I make you nervous?"

"Sometimes."

"Why do ya think that is?"

"I don't know."

"Yes, you fuckin' do," he growled, his lips were on mine before he got the last word out, attacking every last fiber in my being. Never once letting up on his sweet torture of rocking his hard cock against my core.

127

"Who do ya think you're fuckin' with, Pippin? Actin' all grown, when your nothin' but my baby girl. With this pouty little mouth and perfect fuckin' tits, huh? How about that sweet fuckin' pussy? *My sweet fuckin' pussy.*"

My dress was ripped off and discarded on the floor. My bra and panties quickly followed, leaving me bare underneath him. Trying to contain the moan threatening to escape my mouth. He always loved me this way— naked and vulnerable at his mercy when he was still fully clothed. The thought alone made my heart skip a little faster. My insatiable, delicate hands went to his belt, and he shot me a menacing glare as he rapidly flipped me over onto my hands and knees.

Much to my disapproval.

I wanted to see his face, and he knew it. He was punishing me.

"Did I say you could fuckin' touch me? Always doin' what you want, never fuckin' listenin' to a word I say. No matter how many damn times I tell you." I heard his buckle hit the wood floor as he gripped onto my hips. Tossing his shirt aside. Slamming into me in one hard thrust, shoving me forward from the unexpected blow. "Fuck..." he groaned in a low, rumbling tone.

"Yes... yes... yes..." I cried out, swaying my ass, causing his cock to twitch inside of me.

I swear ever since I became pregnant, all I wanted was rough sex. Creed contained the beast inside of himself when it came to us being intimate, which led me to believe I must have pushed him too far over the edge this time. He was going to have his way with me, and I was happily going to let him. Over and over again.

Even if it meant I had to beg to come.

He would let me.

He always did.

Moments later he was thrusting in and out of me in a tortuous rhythm that had me coming undone. I was already wet from earlier, making it easier for his rock hard cock to devour my pussy. I was so wet I could hear the slapping sound of his balls against my ass cheeks with each hard thrust. He leaned forward, brushing my hair to the side of my neck. Giving him access to kiss and lick my heated, overly stimulated skin. His rigid, strong, muscular torso laying heavily on my back as I clawed at the sheets. Imagining it was his tatted flesh.

"Please…" I shamelessly begged, pleading with him to give me what I wanted.

"Please, what, Mia? Tell me what you want, and I might just give it to ya," he taunted, his fingers already slightly moving toward my clit. Leaving nothing but desire and yearning behind. I couldn't hold back any longer, he was purposely trying to drive me insane. I grabbed his fingers, placing them exactly where I wanted them, but he smacked my clit instead.

"Oh God," I panted, my body shivering from the surprise orgasm that coursed through my veins.

"Not God, but damn near close, sweetheart," he snidely chuckled, smacking my clit a few more times. Continuing his assault with his cock deep inside of me.

Caressing.

Manipulating.

Fucking…

Me.

"Please… please… don't stop… please…"

And the bastard pulled out, causing me to whimper from the loss of contact. Thankfully, I didn't have to suffer for very long. He placed my body where he wanted me, sitting right above his mouth. Straddling his handsome, rugged face. Feeling his five o'clock shadow rub against my inner thighs. I could have died of embarrassment from that alone, but I was too far gone to care that we'd never done this before.

"Now is not the time to play shy, babe. I'm fuckin starvin', take a seat on my face and let a man fuckin' eat."

The second I felt him shove his tongue as far into my opening as it could go, I boldly screamed out his name. Two large hands gripped my waist as my body jolted off his mouth, firmly holding me in place. Grinding my hips to sway against his burning tongue.

Eating.

Sucking.

Devouring.

I came again, long and hard. Instantly feeling my wetness slide down the sides of his face. He caressed his large, rough hands up and down the sides of my torso, skimming them up towards my breasts. Kneading, messaging, playing with my nipples.

He pushed two fingers into my pussy, moving them at a rapid speed to make me come even harder. Sending my body into a whirlwind of overwhelming sensations to the point of seeing goddamn stars. Fucking me with his lips, his fingers, giving me everything I wanted and needed and much, much more. My body fell forward, unable to hold myself up any longer. I convulsed all around his fingers. He played with me until I pleaded with him to stop, which only encouraged him to keep going.

CREED

My balls throbbed and my cock ached to be back inside her. I removed my arm from around her leg and slid it down to my cock. Stroking myself to the sounds of her erratic breathing, to the taste of her on my tongue, to the feel of her wrapped around my fucking fingers Letting her ride the fuck out my face, imaging what it would feel like to have her ride my goddamn cock.

Pumping harder and faster, not wanting to stop from eating her sweet, fucking cunt that was dripping down my face. Her bright red clit was sticking out, straight at attention, with her hood fully pulled back. I took it between my pursed lips, in an O shape, and forcefully sucked moving my head side-to-side, humming loud. Fucking her g-spot as she squeezed the fuck out of my face, coming so damn hard, over and over again.

I didn't want her to stop fucking coming.

She gasped for air, trying to catch her bearings. I let her have a few seconds to compose herself before I laid her back down on the bed. Inhaling the sweet, tantalizing smell of her pussy that was all around me as I crawled above her. Stopping when I got to her face.

"You see what's all over my lips? That is mine. Only fuckin' mine."

I grinned, gazing down at her while she peered up at me through dark, hooded eyes. Crudely, I gripped the hair at the nook of her neck with one hand, roughly grabbing onto her ass cheek with the other. Resting one leg over my shoulder. Placing her glistening body where I wanted to so I could thrust into her at a much different angle.

Groaning out, "I'm gonna fuck you now." I slammed into her until I was balls deep, playing with her nipples, taking them into my mouth. Her breathing labored. I rocked my hips back and forth, causing friction on her clit with my lower abdomen as I forcefully fucked her. Mercilessly pounding into her.

"Yes... yes... yes..." she repeated, climaxing all around my fucking shaft. "Oh... my God, oh my God... Creed... I can't... I can't... you're too deep... please..." she cried out, breathless and panting. Clutching onto my hair, her head falling back in ecstasy. Peering at me through slits in her eyes.

"Shhh… you feel so fuckin' good for me this way, baby. So fuckin' good." I bit her neck hard.

Needing to claim her, knowing it would leave a mark, and not giving a flying fuck that it would.

Our mouths parted in unison as I slid in and out of her. She came again, her pussy clamping down on my cock like a goddamn vise. One orgasm rolled over into the next. She couldn't stop coming. Choking the fuck out of my cock, making it almost impossible to not come right with her. I released a loud grunting sound as I spread my seed deep within her core.

We both lay there panting, sweating profusely. Needing air and water. Our hearts beating so loud, you could hear it echoing off the walls.

"I love you," she purred, leaning into my mouth.

I smiled. "I know." Kissing along her lips. "I fuckin' love ya, too."

M. Robinson

the END

You can tell your signficant others…
You're so fucking welcome.

<3 M

45620816R00076

Made in the USA
San Bernardino, CA
12 February 2017